PRAISE FOR THE WORKS OF LAURA ESQUIVEL

LIKE WATER FOR CHOCOLATE

"The most delicious, the most original, the most sumptuous feast of a novel to ever emerge from the kitchens of the New World. *¡Ay que rico!*"

—Sandra Cisneros

"A tall-tale, fairy-tale, soap-opera romance, Mexican cookbook, and home-remedy handbook all rolled into one, *Like Water for Chocolate* is one tasty entree from first-time novelist Laura Esquivel."

—*San Francisco Chronicle*

"Brava Laura Esquivel! This is a truly delicious, funny, sensual, and one-of-a-kind novel that should be required reading for all."

—Diana Kennedy, author of *The Art of Mexican Cooking*

"Esquivel does a splendid job of describing the frustration, love, and hope expressed through the most domestic and feminine of arts, family cooking."

—*Publishers Weekly*

"A mystical Mexican love story [that] will charm the palate and the heart."

—*USA Today*

"A poignant love story."

—*Library Journal*

THE LAW OF LOVE

"How to describe this book? Science fiction? An adventure in a style somewhere between Tom Robbins and Douglas Adams? A mystical study in the likeness of a Jane Roberts Seth book? This cosmic love story is all that and more."

—MostlyFiction.com

"A headlong fantastic adventure-romance full of mystical-moral disquisitions . . . A racy futuristic extravaganza, a romp . . . Her story of two (deeply stupid) twin souls trying to rejoin in love is a crazy, irresponsible comedy, but all through it runs the yearning for a true rejoining, the reconciliation of indio and conquistador, the loving and the murderous, the fleshy and the mystical—all the incompatibles in the great double soul of Mexico."

—Ursula K. Le Guin, *Washington Post* book review

SWIFT AS DESIRE

"Passionate, lyrical, and dramatic, this novel . . . reads smart
and has a big heart."

—*O, The Oprah Magazine*

"Full of passion, fascinating cultural history, and endearing
characters."

—*Library Journal*

"*Swift as Desire* has many charms."

—*New York Times Book Review*

"Esquivel's storytelling abilities are in top form here."

—*Publishers Weekly*

"The love story of Jubilo and Lucha warms the heart."

—*Miami Herald*

"Enchanting and sensuous . . . A beautifully written story
done in [Esquivel's] trademark magical and bittersweet style."

—*Booklist*

"Tender and thoughtful . . . Imaginative, lyrical."

—*Kirkus Reviews*

MALINCHE

"Lyrical."

"[An] amazing story."

"There's something gentle, mystical, yet strong about Laura Esquivel."

"Elegant and simple prose."

"Esquivel puts imaginative flesh on the bones of legend."

"Ambitious and inventive."

PIERCED
by the
SUN

ALSO BY LAURA ESQUIVEL

Like Water for Chocolate

The Law of Love

*Between Two Fires: Intimate Writings
on Life, Love, Food, and Flavor*

Malinche

Swift as Desire

PIERCED

by the

SUN

LAURA
ESQUIVEL

Translated by Jordi Castells

amazon crossing

Text copyright © 2015 Laura Esquivel

Translation copyright © 2016 Jordi Castells

Previously published as *A Lupita le gustaba planchar* by Casa del Libros in Mexico in 2015. Translated from Spanish by Jordi Castells. First published in English by AmazonCrossing in 2016.

Published by AmazonCrossing, Seattle

www.apub.com

Amazon, the Amazon logo, and AmazonCrossing are trademarks of Amazon.com, Inc., or its affiliates.

ISBN-13: 9781503954748
ISBN-10: 1503954749

Cover design by David Drummond

Printed in the United States of America

To the Virgin of Guadalupe

PIERCED
by the
SUN

LUPITA LIKED TO IRON

She could spend long hours dedicated to this work and show no signs of fatigue. Ironing brought her peace. It was her favorite form of therapy and she turned to it daily, even after a long day of work. Lupita's passion for ironing had been handed down to her by her mother, Doña Trini, who had washed and ironed other people's clothes for a living her whole life. Lupita would invariably repeat the ritual learned from her sacrosanct mother, which began with the spraying of the garments. Modern-day steam irons do not require an article of clothing to be moist, but for Lupita there was no other way to iron. She considered it sacrilegious to skip this step.

That night when she got home, she immediately headed to the ironing board and began to spray the garments. Her hands trembled like a hungover alcoholic's, which made the spraying that much easier. It was imperative that she concentrate on something other than the murder of Licenciado Arturo Larreaga—the *delegado* of her district, Iztapalapa—which she had witnessed just a few hours earlier.

As soon as the clothes were properly sprayed she went into the bathroom and turned on the shower, giving the water time to warm up. She filled a bucket with a copious amount of detergent and placed it in the shower. Before she stepped in she opened a plastic bag and immediately recoiled from the stench of the urine-soaked pants that were inside. She submerged the pants in the bucket and started to wash herself. She scrubbed away the cloying smell of urine that had emanated from her body, but the shame that was embedded deep in her soul remained.

What had all those people thought of her when they realized she had pissed herself? What would they think of her now? How could she make them forget the pathetic image of a fat policewoman standing in the middle of a crime scene with dripping pants? As an incorrigible criticizer herself, she was acutely aware of the power an image could have. What she dreaded the most was the thought of Inocencio, the delegado's new driver. Last week she had made such an effort to get his attention, and for what? Now when they ran into each other Inocencio would only remember her in soaking pants. What a way to finally get his attention. Although she had to admit that Inocencio had behaved delicately with her. While she was waiting to give her official statement, she had stepped away from everyone at the precinct in order to not offend them with her stench. When Inocencio approached her, she panicked. The last thing she wanted was for him to smell her! Inocencio was holding a pair of cashmere pants under his arm, explaining that he usually kept them in the trunk of his car. The pants had just been dry-cleaned, and he graciously offered them to Lupita so she could change. He even loaned her his handkerchief so she could dry her tears. She would never, in her whole life, forget this act of tenderness. Ever. But now was not the time to dwell on it, because she could no longer handle the emotional roller coaster she had been on since that morning. Lupita was so tired that the only thing she could do was iron. She stepped out of the shower, dried off vigorously, put on her nightgown, and hurried to turn on her iron.

This ritual helped quiet her thoughts; it would jolt her back into her right mind, as if removing wrinkles were her way of setting the world straight, of asserting her authority. Ironing was an act of annihilation in which wrinkles would die and give way to order: something she required more than anything. She needed to fill her eyes with white, with cleanliness and purity so she could confirm that everything was under control, that there were no loose ends, that the pavement at the corner of Aldama Street and Ayuntamiento Street—right across from Cuihtláhuac Park—wasn't stained with blood.

That was what Lupita yearned for, but instead the white sheets she was ironing became a small movie screen on which images from that afternoon began to play out in front of her eyes.

Lupita saw herself crossing the street across from Cuihtláhuac Park toward the delegado's car. Inocencio was opening the passenger door for his boss. Larreaga was on the phone. Lupita almost bumped into a man while crossing the street, a man who had his hand raised to wave to the delegado. Immediately afterward, Larreaga grasped his neck, which was hemorrhaging blood.

In that moment chaos erupted. Lupita screamed and rushed to the delegado's aid, unable to make sense of what had just happened. Nobody had shot at the delegado. There was no explosion. There was no evidence of anybody in the vicinity having any sort of knife or blade; nevertheless, a sharp object must have caused the wound to the jugular that bled Licenciado Larreaga dry. The more Lupita struggled to understand what had happened, the more she doubted everything. The more she tried to forget the look of surprise in Larreaga's eyes when he received the wound that would take his life, the stronger it replayed in her mind and caused her to feel nausea, tremors, anguish, discomfort, rage, indignation . . . and fear. Tremendous fear.

Lupita knew fear. She had felt it thousands of times before. She could smell it, perceive it, and predict it in herself or in others. Like a stray dog, she could detect it from a distance. She could tell if people were afraid of being robbed or raped by the way they walked. She could tell who was afraid of being discriminated against, who feared old age, poverty, or being kidnapped. But there was nothing more transparent to her than the fear of not being loved, the fear of being unseen, of being ignored. That was her greatest fear, and she now felt it deep in her bones in spite of having been the center of attention for several hours. In spite of appearing all over the news as the main witness to what the media were calling a political murder. In spite of her testimony being the only thing that could lead authorities to the perpetrator. Lupita had been pressured and rushed into giving her version of events. She'd felt forced to declare the first thing that came to mind so she would not seem like an incompetent fool who had not seen or heard anything, all of which magnified her fear of being ridiculed.

She even heard a television anchorman—referring to the fact that she had wet her pants—exclaim: "That's what happens when you give a badge to a maid." Asshole! Who did he think he was? The worst thing was that the comment actually got to her. It hurt her deeply. It cornered her as a third-class citizen. It catalogued her within a group of people who'd never be loved or admired even when they had stood in the eye of the hurricane. Nothing had spared her from being mocked for wetting her pants, not even the fact that she had rushed to the delegado's aid. What bothered her most was the officer who'd taken her statement and his smug look when she mentioned that it might be important that a wrinkle had disappeared from the delegado's shirt collar. Lupita felt she had not explained herself correctly. She had not been able to convey the importance of that wrinkle—a wrinkle that had been very clearly evident on his collar earlier that morning at the adult education center but was completely gone after he was murdered. In her opinion this opened a possible line of investigation.

The feeling of having made a fool of herself was eating at her from the inside. Her face was flushed and a fire burned deep within her. The discomfort was so great that not even two hours of ironing calmed her. Both her mind and the iron wandered aimlessly. Lupita wasn't even aware of how clumsily and abruptly she was ironing. She slid the iron over the fabric without her usual finesse and created new wrinkles, which in turn forced her to spray more to get rid of the fresh markings. The steam that emanated as a result was irritating and increased the stifling sensation inside her. An incredible amount of shame was growing and spinning wildly in her chest. There were no words to describe what she felt; it was something similar to heartburn. It was a destructive fire that made her want to leave her body, to get away from herself before being engulfed in flames. Her heart was beating rapidly, out of control. Her hands went numb. She wished to escape this world, to be somewhere else, but at the same time she was terrified of dying. Her breathing was shallow, and she felt like she could lose her mind at any moment and go completely insane. Lupita turned off the iron and set it aside. She needed to alleviate some of her pain urgently or she would burst from sheer anguish.

To top it all off, her AA sponsor wasn't picking up the phone. Lupita had left several voicemails, but he wasn't calling back. He had probably gone on vacation because of the long weekend. She had a list of other AA members she could turn to for help, but no one was taking her call. Fucking holidays! Fucking country! Fucking TV news anchormen! Fucking corrupt politicians! This is what they had come to in order to prevent Licenciado Larreaga from interfering with their plans! Fucking thugs! Fucking narcos! And fucking gringo drug addicts! If they didn't consume most of the drugs produced in the world, there wouldn't be so many Mexican drug cartels trying to satiate their demand! Fucking narco-governments! If they weren't so hungry for illegal money siphoned off from drug trafficking, there wouldn't be so much death! Fucking chickenshit legislators! If only they had the balls to legalize drugs. Then there wouldn't be so much organized crime or so much fucking ambition for easy money! We wouldn't be in this state of disarray, damn it! And fucking God, who was so fucking distracted for some reason! Lupita cursed and cursed until there was no one left to curse, including herself, because in the past she had protected small-time drug dealers to ensure she got her fix.

For a split second she felt inclined to go out and get a bottle of tequila, but the memory of her dead son held her back. Lupita had sworn on his grave that she would never drink again, and she intended to keep that promise. She tried, and failed, to remember her child's face. It was a blur. It seemed to purposely evade her. Trying to recall the sound of his childish laughter produced the same empty result. It was as if it had never registered in her memory. Her memory operated in a strange manner. Who knows what it obeyed—certainly not Lupita. Worse still, it was her best weapon for self-harm. She could only remember things that hurt, that tortured her, that made her feel like the worst woman—the worst mother—in the world. She couldn't even recall happy and luminous events without connecting them to painful and devastating ones. After a great deal of effort, Lupita was able to recall the color of her son's eyes, and his innocent gaze came to her mind as well as his expression of utter shock when she— completely intoxicated—landed the blow that had accidentally taken his life. She doubled up with pain. A wave of guilt crashed over her and sent her reeling to the floor, howling like a wounded animal.

That night, for the first time in her life, Lupita left wrinkled clothes on the ironing board.

LUPITA LIKED BOOZE

Boy, did she like it! She liked to drink until she was completely lost. What she liked the most about drinking was
not being present, that feeling of self-evasion, of disconnection, of liberation, of escape. Alcohol offered her an
excellent alternative to being herself without actually
dying. She just banished the rest of the world from her
sight and thus put an end to her suffering. In other words
alcohol absolutely anesthetized her. As a young girl all she

had to do to evade her problems was center her attention on the motions of a small spider or an ant, but as she got older simple contemplation stopped being enough. How did she choose alcohol? She couldn't remember. Her contact with alcohol began at an early age. It was the most ubiquitous substance in her family and social environments. There wasn't a single party or celebration where booze wasn't flowing. The first time she got drunk she only noticed the benefits. Maybe she was attracted to her stepfather's change in personality when he came home tipsy. He was generally a silent, reserved man with a tough demeanor, but when he drank he turned into a cheerful, likable chatterbox with a mischievous gleam in his eyes.

On those days she had enjoyed being around him because normally her stepfather ignored her completely and only communicated with her via monosyllabic grunts. But when he was drunk he ruffled her hair and joked around with her. They laughed together, something she greatly enjoyed. On those days she loved alcohol. Lupita always tried to have a cold beer waiting for her stepfather when he came home from work. But her perception of alcohol changed drastically the night her stepfather came home completely wasted and raped her. That night she hated alcohol. She hated the lingering smell of her stepfather's body and the destructive capacity of the substance. From that day on her relationship with booze fluctuated between love and hate.

The rape had transformed her into a shy, sullen, ill-tempered girl who no longer wanted to be touched, kissed, or caressed. Lupita no longer danced, sang, or enjoyed life. She isolated herself from everyone until Manolo walked through the door of her apartment building's Christmas party. She'd had a huge crush on her neighbor, and that day seeing him made her wish with all her heart to be someone else, to transform into an amiable, adventurous, and sensual teenage queen of the night who could seduce the love of her life. Lupita had decided alcohol would help her achieve this. She was so tired of being the sad girl on the block. Without a second thought she had a drink, and then another, and then another. Her best friend, Celia, had advised Lupita to slow down. Fortunately Lupita obeyed and interrupted her alcohol consumption just in time. She didn't get properly drunk, just buzzed enough to reach her objective: Lupita, without a doubt, was the life of that party. She smiled, she joked, and she danced like crazy. Everyone was surprised because Lupita didn't usually dance in public, as she was mortally afraid of being stared at and judged, of her feet missing a beat and causing her to stand out like a sore thumb. She couldn't bear the thought of being mocked by her peers. But that night Manolo asked her to dance. They were the hottest couple at the party, and for days afterward the only thing her neighbors could talk about was how hot Lupita had looked and what a good dancer she was.

In Lupita's mind alcohol became her best ally, her passport to freedom. It gave her access to a world where the fear of being seen, of being touched, of being raped again did not exist.

Manolo had asked Lupita to be his girlfriend during the party, and it was under the effects of alcohol that Lupita received her first kiss and her first caresses, and experienced her first vaginal wetness. From that day on she turned to alcohol every time she needed to feel brave. Three drinks were enough to make her feel like the happiest, most sensual woman. She felt like number one! Never mind that she inhabited a short, chubby body.

The night of her fifteenth birthday, her mother threw her an unforgettable party. Doña Trini had saved for many years in order to throw the *quinceañera* party of her daughter's dreams. She rented a ballroom and bought Lupita a puffy tulle dress that made her look fatter than she actually was. When Lupita saw herself in the dress she knew she would not be able to face her family and friends without the help of tequila. Before her big dance she hid in a bathroom stall and chugged half a bottle.

Lupita remembered her grand entrance in front of all her guests and nothing more. She had blacked out. To this day she couldn't recall the slightest detail from the dance. She didn't know if she had messed up, or if Manolo had stepped on her foot. Her mind had gone blank. Days later her mother commented how sweet it was that Lupita had cried "tears of joy" when she danced with her stepfather. But Lupita knew that if any tears had escaped her eyes they were surely caused by the revulsion and shame of being in her stepfather's embrace.

The only memory she had of that night was embedded in her mind months later, when her doctor had informed her she was pregnant. It was then that she learned what the indiscriminate use of alcohol could cause. That was when everything spiraled out of control. That was when her life changed completely. Nevertheless, even though Lupita knew how alcohol had destroyed her life and her family and romantic relationships, she still yearned to get a good buzz. She urgently needed a drink. Hell, not one, several drinks. She no longer cared about the consequences or the hangover. Right then and there she would have given anything to be able to drink herself to death. Or at least drink herself into a stupor so this hellish night would finally end.

LUPITA LIKED TO WASH

She loved to put her hands in the water and repeat her
mantra: "Just for today. Just for today I will choose water
over alcohol. Just for today I will allow water to cleanse
me, to purify me." Lupita liked living sober. But that
clarity made her extremely anxious because she knew she
had done so many things she couldn't remember, things
that would cause her much more guilt if she could actually recall them. She would never wish her blackouts on

anyone—waking up in some hotel naked, raped, beaten, or in the middle of the street, stripped of all possessions. One of the steps in the Alcoholics Anonymous program was to seek forgiveness and try to repair damages. Lupita had covered this step to the best of her knowledge, but what about the times she had no clue about what she had done, or whom she had hit or insulted? Not to mention maybe having robbed, assaulted, or stabbed someone. But after a session at the washbasin she would feel like her guilt had gone down the drain along with the dirt in her clothes. This is where she confessed her conscious and unconscious sins and let them go down the drain. Without knowing the details she could sense a sacred presence in the water and knew that in her reflection she could find a pure, clean version of herself.

So Lupita bowed to that invisible presence, imploring clarity. She didn't want to relapse into drinking. She wanted to choose water as her patron, as her protector, as her mistress.

TLAZOLTÉOTL

Tlazoltéotl was an Aztec goddess. She was classified by the Spaniards as the "Eater of Ordure," although recent research into the pre-Hispanic spiritual world reveals her as a fertility deity that was present in all aspects of life, from birth to death, including resurrection. For each stage of life she had a different name and represented a distinct process, but her presence within temples and in rituals was essential to guaranteeing the conservation of life. During birth, the deity participated as the great purifier. During terrestrial life she was known as the Goddess of Knitters, those who covered, those who clothed. During death she was accompanied by the *Cihuateteo* (women who had died during childbirth) as she escorted the sun

through its path in the heavens and helped
it be reborn. She had a temple where men
confessed their sins, which when forgiven
became light and renewed life. That was
her real purpose: to make fertilizer out of
that which had been discarded.

Lupita couldn't help but wonder if someone had washed
the delegado's blood off of the pavement. Where had that
water flowed?

The thought of the delegado's blood running down
the drain made her ponder the cold-blooded indifference
of nature's actions. After the cleanup crew was done, that
was that! Water solves problems. Water dilutes, cleans,
purifies. After the street was washed, pedestrians would
have no clue that a murder had taken place there. Water
had no need to go after the guilty, to seek them out or
judge and condemn them. Water operated by different
laws and Lupita liked how it litigated. The washbasin's

justice system was relentless and democratic. Clothes could not be corrupted. Water and soap could put an end to the worst filth without bothering with any petty interests. And after a proper ironing, there was not a single trace of disorder. Something Lupita often thought when she was done washing: "Render unto the earth what is the earth's and render unto the sun what is the sun's." In the case of the delegado's blood, she wondered what part of it belonged to the earth and what part to the sun. It wasn't clear. The essence of the blood would travel in the water and eventually evaporate. In that steamy state it would reach the sky and return to the earth again in the form of rain. It would be present both in the memory of the sky and in the memory of the earth.

This reflection troubled Lupita's soul. She was washing the pants that she had soaked in the bucket of soapy water the previous night. Traces of her urine and the delegado's blood had permeated the fabric. This combination of fluids would travel through the drain in unison and the water would contain the memory of them both. On the one hand, water washed away the evidence of what had transpired, but on the other hand, it transported the delegado's and Lupita's essences, and Lupita didn't want to remain in the water's memory under such conditions. She wanted to be swallowed by the earth and to remain in darkness long enough to feel new. She didn't want to share her shame with anyone. She wanted to travel down the drain and through the pipes without being noticed, to snuggle in the arms of the magnificent Grandmother in an underground cave where no one could see her, where she could exist in peace and without judgment. It was easy to remove traces of urine and blood from clothes, but it was more complicated to dispel them from memory. They were embedded in Lupita's memory, and there was no way to eliminate them. "Just for today," Lupita said. "Just for today I will let water purify me." Yet the images of what she had witnessed still did not disappear from her mind, from her skin, from her nose, or from her eyes in spite of being so tired that it was hard to focus her vision on the pants she was vigorously washing in the washbasin.

However, her prayer was heard, and the water took a detour down the drain. Just like the ocean tides answer the moon's calling, so did the drain water answer Lupita's petition. It exited the drain through a miniscule leak in the pipes that connected Lupita's building to the sewage line, and it impregnated the earth. When the soil was moist enough, the water seeped down into an underground cave where it fell drip by drip. A very important ceremony had taken place there three nights before.

Three nights before . . . under a full moon, Concepción Ugalde's face looked spectral, illuminated by the torch she held in her hand. Doña Concepción was a shaman, widely respected by the council of elders in her community. To them she was better known as Conchita. She was a woman of undecipherable age, with a kind face and long gray braids. Her feet slowly slid along the rocks inside an abandoned underground cave. The white walls had been formed thousands of years back by runoff from underground rivers high in calcium carbonate. In time, the constant flow of water had formed petrified waterfalls. Conchita was escorted by men and women who walked behind her in complete silence and in a straight line, each one of them carrying a torch. They walked along a tunnel until they reached a wide chamber shaped like a half-moon. The place was a wonder to behold. Imposing. Water spouted from the white rocks of its surface and fed into four springs, each of which pointed toward one of the four cardinal points. The water from the springs flowed down a channel to the center of the chamber where all four streams congregated, forming a sacred well. The water swirled as it flowed to the center, giving off a pleasant aroma.

A stone staircase with thirteen steps descended down each slope toward the well. Conchita climbed down and entered the water. From a pouch that hung from her neck, she produced a small circular piece of obsidian, and she raised it toward the sky. In that instant a small ray of moonlight shone through a crack in the cave and illuminated the stone Conchita held between her fingers. The rest of the people began to chant as a young man joined Conchita in the water and received the stone. His name was Tenoch, and his black eyes shone as bright as the obsidian. His earlobes were stretched with gauges, and he had a labret piercing—all three pieces of jewelry made of the same volcanic material. Conchita said to him, "May the light shine strongly through the darkness in which our people have fallen. May our warriors triumph over the forces that prevent us from seeing our true face in the face of our brothers. Lord Quetzalcóatl, you who purified your bodily matter and set it ablaze to become the Morning Star, you who faced the black mirror and found liberation from its deceitful reflection, help us free the spirit of our people so we can look upon the rebirth of the Fifth Sun with refreshed eyes."

Lupita, of course, had no idea about the underground chamber where the water from the washbasin flowed after it went down the drain, or about the events that had transpired in it three nights earlier. Her mind was in a state of confusion. She still couldn't even focus her eyes. They felt like there was sand in them because she hadn't slept at all. This had definitely been the second worst night of her life. The worst night of her life was when she had accidentally killed her son. When she saw the toddler fall to the floor and not get up, Lupita set her bottle aside and fell to her knees beside him. She took her son's flaccid body in her arms and realized he was dead.

Lupita had held him in her arms firmly and didn't let go all night. She didn't budge a fraction of an inch from the position she settled in, and she was unable to remove her gaze from the boy's face. Her son's body lost warmth and got rigid, and so did hers. And just like she had practiced throughout her childhood, she tried to evade the moment by concentrating on an external event. As moonlight had entered the room through a window that was right behind her head Lupita carefully observed how her own shadow drew a half-moon shape on her son's face. As the night wore on, she had all the time in the world to observe how that shadow changed.

At first it had covered just his eyes and forehead, but later the shadow bathed the boy's face in black, only to slowly recede and become a partial eclipse once more. Lupita concentrated her thoughts on lunar eclipses. She thought that maybe Galileo Galilei had lost a child in his arms just like her, on a night just as sad as this one, and thus had discovered that only a round shape that comes between the sun and the moon can project a circular shadow, providing irrefutable proof that the earth is round and that it orbits the sun.

For the whole night she had not allowed her mind to dwell on anything other than the trajectory of the planets in the cold quiet of space. She also thought about how the earth gets cold when it's not in direct sunlight, and how the cold disappears when the sun rises again over the horizon. But that night—the worst night of her life—Lupita knew that warmth would never return to her body. Not the next morning, or the next day, or the next week or month, because she understood that she had just murdered the sun.

It took her a long time to be able to sleep at night again, and a lot longer for her body to recover the warmth she had lost. When she went to prison, the walls of her cell felt warm compared to her cold skin.

LUPITA LIKED TO FEEL SORRY FOR HERSELF

Of course she was not aware of it. Her thoughts and feelings perfectly fit the psychological description of a victim suffering from seriously low self-esteem. She had been convinced of her own worthlessness for so many years that she irrevocably placed herself below others, thus obeying an unconscious desire to feel insignificant. That was how she was brought up, and that was how she had lived her whole life. Her deep and hidden thoughts had been in control of her existence for years and would only emerge at the most critical times with the intention of re-creating ad nauseam what it meant to live a life of misery. For that matter, she had no memory of having experienced even a glimmer of well-being in her entire life.

"Poor me" was the phrase that came to her mind repeatedly, as a choir of imaginary mariachis responded "Oh, my heart!" And again "Poor me," and then the chorus: "Suffer no more." The lyrics and tune belonged to a song performed by Pedro Infante. Lupita wondered why tragedy had knocked on her door once more. Why hadn't she stopped for a couple of minutes at the diner where she usually used the bathroom during her rounds? What might have happened if she had disobeyed her doctor's orders to drink almost a gallon of water every day to alleviate her urinary problems? She rapidly came to the conclusion that even if she had not pissed her pants, some other horrible thing would have happened. She just couldn't win. Everything seemed to be stacked against her. What would have happened if instead of being four feet nine she were five feet eleven? She might have been assigned to the touristy parts of town, like the Zona Rosa. What if instead of weighing 160 pounds she weighed 120? She could have been a game-show girl on *En Familia con Chabelo*. What if she had passed the GED when she joined the police? What if her stepfather hadn't raped her? What if her husband hadn't beaten her so many times? What kind of life would she have now? A different one, that was for sure.

First of all, she wouldn't be washing her clothes by hand at the crack of dawn so she could avoid her neighbors, who would very likely bombard her with questions about the delegado's unusual death. Of course, her unusual timing backfired and caused exactly what she had meant to avoid. The splashing of the water as she furiously scrubbed woke everyone in her building. She could hear Doña Chencha—a voice coach for street vendors—clear her throat with gargles earlier than she usually did. She heard Don Simon flush his toilet and she heard the unmistakable creak of Celia's door opening.

Lupita rinsed her pants in a hurry to avoid Celia. As she was wringing them she felt a splinter pierce her finger. The fear of facing her neighbor was suddenly unimportant, because the blood from the wound prevented her from figuring out what type of splinter it was. Lupita was sucking on her wounded finger, trying to remove the splinter via suction, when Celia appeared on the patio with an offering for Lupita: a cup of guava *atole* and a *tamal torta*. Lupita broke down in tears. She was deeply stirred, knowing that her experience the previous day could have such an effect on Celia. They hugged, and Celia also broke down in tears as an act of solidarity to her friend. *This is quite the act of love*, Lupita thought, and not because of the tears. Celia usually woke up late in the day, but today she had gotten up before dawn and had overcome her vanity, stepping out of her house without doing her hair and makeup. All to go out and buy Lupita her favorite breakfast.

Of course, when Lupita saw that Celia was also carrying a copy of the notorious tabloid *El Metro*, it became clear that her gossipy friend didn't want to just comfort her. She wanted to know more about the bizarre circumstances surrounding the delegado's death. Her curiosity had to be infinite, because not even when María "La Doña" Félix died had Celia gotten up early to question

Lupita about the details, even though she knew Lupita was assigned as security detail at the funeral and had been in the presence of a number of celebrities.

"Did you see yourself on the cover?" Celia asked.

Lupita didn't want to know anything, or see anything for that matter, but Celia shoved the front page in her face. While doing so, Celia noticed that Lupita stained the newspaper with blood as she held it. She asked what had happened, and Lupita explained that it was just a splinter. Celia immediately offered to help. She took her friend by the hand and dragged her back into her apartment, where she had every tool necessary for the extraction—scissors, tweezers, magnifying glass—plus a manicure set and a waxing toolkit, both of which Celia also pulled out.

"Damn, *mana*! This is a glass shard! Damn, these are hard to get out."

"A glass shard? How? Are you sure it isn't wood? Look, it's kind of dark."

"No, mana, here's a piece. Look at it through the magnifying glass."

Indeed, it was a glass shard, and it very probably came from the scene of the crime. Lupita's mind raced back to the attack, and she remembered that when she knelt to help Larreaga, she picked up the cell phone he had dropped and put it in her pocket to ensure no one would steal it. There was always that one asshole who would try to take advantage of the situation. The screen was completely shattered, and that was surely where the shard had come from.

Pain brought her back to the present. The procedure her finger was undergoing was extremely painful. Nevertheless, Lupita found a certain comfort in it. You could say pain was her thing and Celia was a part of that. They had grown up together, and Celia had been a witness to everything Lupita had suffered, so the combination of Celia, pain, and blood was one of the constants in her life. It was a package deal. Celia also brought another component to the table: gossip, rumors, the voice of the neighborhood. Lupita knew from experience that it was best to satiate Celia's thirst for information or she would lose a finger. So she finally gave Celia her account of the previous day, not without being constantly interrupted by her friend's impertinent questions.

"Tell me everything! Was it horrible, mana?"

"Yeah, you can't imagine the face he made. He looked at me like begging for help and . . ."

"Was that when you pissed yourself?"

"I think so, I don't remember . . . I . . ."

"But tell me, how did they kill him? Who slashed his throat?"

"Well, I don't know . . ."

"C'mon, mana, don't give me that! Weren't you standing a few feet from him?"

"Yeah, but I swear, it's all so weird. No one even came near him. The only one who was remotely close to him was his driver."

"The new one? The one you have a crush on?"

Lupita nodded.

"Well, isn't *he* the killer?"

"No way!"

If only Lupita hadn't been on duty! Even better: if only she had never been born! Or at least died years before. Before she became a mother. Before she became an alcoholic. Before she killed her son. Before she had been in prison. Before bearing witness to electoral fraud. Before witnessing so many fucking murders. Before her country was taken over by the drug cartels. Before Celia massacred her hand trying to extract a goddamned glass shard.

"I'm sorry, mana, am I hurting you?"

"Yes. Can't you get it out without cutting me up?"

"It's really deep and won't come out. Look, it breaks when I try to pull it out."

Every time Celia managed to latch on to the tip of the glass, it broke off and the rest of the shard dug deeper.

"But tell me, is it true that it might have been the chupacabra?"

"Jesus, Celia!"

Lupita was done with talking. More accurately she was done with trying to talk, because Celia hadn't let her finish a single sentence. On top of that she felt like she neither knew nor understood anything, except that her life had changed. The feeling of having no control over the world and the situations surrounding her was perplexing. The only thing she could perceive was that everything she planned, everything she struggled for, was doomed to failure. She couldn't help but compare that look on the delegado's face to the look on her son's face when she killed him. She wept.

She cried not only for her dead son, for herself, and for the delegado, but for all that could have been, everything that never grew, all that never was. She cried for all the corn that would never grow because farmers got paid more for their crops if they planted opium poppies. She cried with rage over the approval of an energetic reform that opened the doors for foreign investors to take over Mexican oil. Lupita took the approval of that reform as a personal affront. She had been born on December 12, the day of the Virgin of Guadalupe, whom she was named after. The Mexican Congress had approved the reform that same day. Lupita considered the entire ordeal treason to the nation, to the Virgin, and to herself because from that day on her birthday would be stained by that humiliating act. Lupita also cried for a Mexico that was in the hands of traitors, drug cartels, and murderers who killed people like her, and people like the delegado.

She also cried for the fate of an entire *delegación*, now in nefarious hands. It would surely be overrun by one of the groups that represented the most corrupt and petty interests of a political party that called itself leftist but had dealings with the most extreme right wing. The delegado's death meant the death of new possibilities. Lupita cried and cried for him and his large eyes and clean gaze.

Lupita had followed the delegado since his first campaign. He had been a decent man who had really tried to change things but wasn't allowed. He wasn't corrupt. From the beginning of his administration he faced off against the mafias that ran Delegación Iztapalapa: neighborhood leaders, congressmen, religious leaders—those who only worked for their own personal benefit and didn't give a rat's ass about Mexico. The worst among them were the ones who betrayed their own people. Like the ones who stole the eyeglasses the government handed out for free and then resold them to the poor. Or the ones who bought votes to ensure the triumph of a candidate who would look after their private business without caring what happened to the rest of the neighborhood. The ones who didn't let their own people live decent lives. Those who took control by force, threatened others, and killed any possibility of change. Lupita knew them. She had seen them in action, she had heard them at their political meetings, and she had seen them betray even their own mothers in order to get ahead.

She thought nothing more could surprise her, and yet here she was, completely surprised. She thought nothing new could scare her, yet she was terrified. She thought nothing else could humiliate her, and she felt like shit. She thought nothing else could hurt her, yet she ached deep inside. She thought this March would be over without claiming another victim, yet the heartless month had dealt another deadly blow. Every big tragedy in Lupita's life had happened in the month of March: she had brutally lost her virginity, her mother, her son, her innocence, even Selena, her favorite singer. Huge losses.

"We all think it was Ostión," said Celia, yanking Lupita back into the present. "Remember he got in a fight with the delegado the day before yesterday?"

"What? Who told you that?"

"I heard it from the delegado's wife. Selene Larreaga called me soon after her husband's murder. She wanted to get her nails done."

"She called you to make a manicure appointment after she learned of her husband's death?"

"Yes, mana, and to be honest with you, I understand her. She had a broken nail! She couldn't go on the news like that! But she was also really sad and nervous, trust me! She told me we had plenty of time for her manicure because it was gonna take a while for the cops to clear the crime scene, move the body, and perform an autopsy."

LUPITA LIKED TO BE A BITCH

Not always, only when she was drunk. And not to everyone, only to those who belittled her. It hurt so much to
be cast aside and ignored that at the slightest provocation
she lashed back automatically. She was capable of uttering
every insult that came to mind at an unheard of speed
just to feel superior to her attackers. In the end, what
she sought from them was a look of respect instead of a

look of contempt, which to this day had not happened once. To the contrary, she got sloppier and sloppier during her fits of rage and people would do anything to avoid her when she had been drinking, fearsome of her viper tongue.

Lupita was currently making a great effort to suppress her anger. She was biting her lips as she waited in the hall of the delegación offices to elaborate on her statement. Captain Martinez, the officer in charge of the investigation, had called her in to corroborate some of her stated facts. As she waited, she couldn't help but to mentally criticize and insult everyone that averted their gaze or greeted her with a mocking smirk.

Lupita was very upset. Really angry. Pissed off. She sensed the atmosphere of hostility, and she could feel herself slipping into her mean-drunk mode. Before heading to the government offices she had downed a fifth of tequila. That was the only way she could show her face after yesterday's events. She couldn't handle this kind of pressure sober.

Lupita wasn't the only one on the brink of a rage attack. The general mood was tense. No one had the slightest clue how the delegado had been killed. Everybody showed signs of fatigue. No one had slept the previous night. Lupita had at least had time to go home and shower, unlike the others. She understood their irritation, but nothing excused the looks of disgust directed toward her. Especially Chief Arévalo, who walked past her without even acknowledging her presence when, just two days before, he had his way with her in a bathroom at the police station. Lupita let him do what he wanted in exchange for a favor. Her work schedule was a twenty-four-hour shift followed by twenty-four hours off. But since she wanted to be part of the traffic detail at the grand opening for an adult education center where the delegado would make a speech, she allowed the abuse. Why? Simply put, she'd wanted a chance to get close to Inocencio Corona, whom she had fallen for the first instant she had laid eyes on him. She urgently wanted to strike up a friendship with him, and what better opportunity than to spend some time with him while the delegado inaugurated the school. That old pig Arévalo had changed her shift in exchange for groping her in the bathroom, and was now not only ignoring her but also looking down at her with disdain. Who did that asshole think he was? He was walking to and fro with an air of importance, pretending he had things under control when in reality everything was a mess.

The government offices at Delegación Iztapalapa swarmed with people coming in and out, going up and down, arguing, demanding attention. The delegado's death could not have come at a worse time. Iztapalapa was only days away from the Easter celebrations, and the local reenactment of the Passion of the Christ was quite an event. The tradition began in 1843 and with the passing of time had become the world's biggest mass theater, thanks to the participation of over five hundred local performers. Throughout the year men, women, and children prepared intensely for the festivity. On Good Friday everyone took to the streets and, dressed as Nazarenes, they escorted the actor portraying Christ along a lengthy tour that came to an end at the foot of Star Hill, site of the crucifixion. The pre-Hispanic remains at Star Hill form part of an architectural complex. At the top stands a pyramid where the New Fire was lit every fifty-two years.

THE LIGHTING OF THE NEW FIRE

The ancient people of Tenochtitlán believed that once every fifty-two years a cosmic cycle ended and gave way to a new one. The sun was the main protagonist. On these special nights they believed that when the sun set it would never rise again. So they enacted a ceremony that—according to the historians of the conquest—coincided with the night the Pleiades star cluster reached the highest point in the sky. When night fell, priests adorned with their gods' insignias would march to the top of Huizache Hill, currently known as Star Hill. All fires in the city were put out and families would clean out their houses and destroy all common household items. A fire was started at the top of the hill and the priests lit torches

that were handed over to the fastest run-
ner so they could spread the New Fire.
The indigenous peoples believed that the
hill and the sun in unison were the repre-
sentation of God. When Friar Bernardino
de Sahagún learned of this ritual, he integrated the symbolism in the leaflets he
used to convert natives to Catholicism.

Everyone from big-shot TV producers to street vendors
was gathered at the Delegación Iztapalapa offices. They
were all worried that the murder would cause the Passion
procession to be canceled. There were many interests at
stake: the television networks complained that crime-
scene investigators interfered with the placement of their
cameras, street vendors refused to remove their booths
from Cuihtláhuac Park, and government authorities were
trying to convince them that they had to clear a path
for the procession. They argued that before his untimely

death the delegado had authorized them to set up their booths in the park. And just like the street vendors, many others claimed to have secured verbal agreements with the delegado, which they worried would not be followed through. Licenciado Buenrostro, the legal and government affairs director of the delegación, was the man in charge of meeting with—and defusing—the dissatisfied citizens. Buenrostro's face was set in a permanent scowl, and he had quite a reputation for shutting down businesses and then collecting bribes to let them operate again.

One of the principal complainers was Mami, the leader of the street vendors, who loudly demanded that her booths be allowed to remain at the park. Mami had her differences with the delegado since it was common knowledge that some of the vendors she represented sold cheap Chinese knockoffs as well as drugs. Lupita knew most of these vendors by name because in her years as an addict she had copped from them.

Mami gave Lupita the chills. She was a heartless woman known to put out hits on people who opposed her plans. She extorted left and right. Her power was such that the delegación always consulted her on the handling of budgets for social programs. She would even give orders to policemen, treating them like her personal servants. Once, Mami tried to make Lupita run an errand for her, and Lupita had refused. Mami had been livid, but no violent consequences had befallen Lupita. She had come to the conclusion that she was insignificant to Mami.

Whispers and rumors abounded in the hallways of the delegación offices. The delegado's strange death gave free rein to wild speculation. Some said the delegado had argued with Mami over the removal of a group of street vendors. Some said Congressman Francisco Torreja—known as Ostión because he was slimy and slippery like an oyster—had sent death threats to the delegado because the latter had planned to file a corruption case against the former. Ostión was definitely the most corrupt congressman Lupita had ever met. The son of a bitch threatened his female constituents, bought favors, protected drug dealers, and was now a constant presence at the delegado's former office, trying to take advantage of the mass confusion.

Another sketchy character that was subject to suspicion was Licenciado Hilario Gomez, the delegado's chief advisor. Everyone was talking about the public screaming match they'd gotten into the day before. Hilario had been late to an event where the delegado had to give an annual status report. One of the secretaries told Lupita that what had angered the delegado most was the fact that Hilario refused to give a reason as to why he was late or where he had been. He had not even sent the PowerPoint presentation deck beforehand, so the delegado had been forced to improvise.

Lupita thought Hilario was a wily, two-faced, corrupt liar. She had never liked him in the slightest. He was one of those people who never looked you in the eye. She had never seen him laugh. He was a clammy-handed, four-eyed, bald, fat-ass yes-man who distilled envy and profound ambition. He said he was a leftist but that was a lie. Money was the only thing he cared about. He was a lonely man, never known to have a girlfriend, wife, partner, or even a pet. He was usually tangled up in strategies and planning that proved counterproductive to the delegado's agenda. Lupita never understood why the delegado kept him around. Maybe because of a political arrangement? It didn't matter. She couldn't stand the fucker.

Just as someone was elaborating on the motives he may have had to kill the delegado, Hilario entered the building. A dead silence fell upon the hallway. Everyone was quiet, with the exception of Lupita. And everybody's jaws dropped when she loudly and disrespectfully asked, "Why don't you tell all these people who are bad-mouthing you that you were late for the delegado's report because you were getting your back waxed?"

That was true, actually. Hilario's cause for tardiness was a cosmetic hair removal appointment. How did Lupita know this? Because Celia had told her in confidence. She had personally handled the waxing procedure and even confided that she had singed his skin a bit because he was in a hurry and asked her to apply the wax when it was still too hot. He mentioned being late for an important event.

"If he was in such a hurry to be at work, why the fuck was he getting his back waxed?" Lupita had asked Celia.

"I think it's because he's going to the beach with a lady friend over the weekend and that was the only free time he could find to get rid of his back hair."

"Yuck. Who would want to sleep with that guy?"

"Don't take this the wrong way, mana, but some say that it is the delegado's wife . . ."

"Stop Celia! Shut up, I just threw up in my mouth a little."

Everyone in the hallway held their breath.

"Why don't you also tell everyone that you would be incapable of killing your friend and boss over work issues. But you totally would do it just to sleep with his wife."

At that very moment, as if by divine intervention, Lupita was called into the captain's office. Hilario stood in shock, having missed his chance to pounce on her.

"Good morning, Captain."

"Take a seat please."

The captain's office was tight and his desk was small, so Lupita's face was quite close to his when she sat down and mumbled a thank-you.

"I didn't know you could show up for duty with alcohol on your breath. Do you always come to work like this?"

"No, not always. Why?"

"As far as I know you can't drink while on duty."

"You're right. But don't worry, I'm not on duty today," Lupita said arrogantly. "How can I be of service? I already gave a thorough statement yesterday."

Captain Martinez smiled, surprised by Lupita's attitude. In his hands he held a transcript of Lupita's official account of the events in question. "Yes, I've reviewed it. By the way, I wanted to ask you about the wrinkle you mentioned in your statement. What exactly do you mean by that?"

Lupita fidgeted in her seat. The question unnerved her. She couldn't figure out the captain's intention in asking her this.

"Well, it was similar to the one on your shirt collar, except yours isn't the result of improper ironing. It seems like when you folded your shirt you did so carelessly and the collar was squashed."

"Go on. I'm interested."

"Look, hands also iron. Sometimes it's not enough to iron a piece of clothing, it also has to be folded properly and with the right amount of pressure, smoothing out all creases. Oh, and you shouldn't leave your jacket on the same sofa where your cat sleeps because its hair sticks to it."

Captain Martinez couldn't help but show an admiration that illuminated his eyes. This woman's words were the most refreshing thing he had heard in a long time. He watched as Lupita mimicked the action of flicking cat hair off her shoulder, and he noticed that she grimaced when her wounded finger brushed against her clothing.

"What happened there?"

"Nothing important, just a splinter."

"Judging from the wound it looks like a big one."

"I know, right? But don't worry, it's got nothing to do with the investigation. Now back to the wrinkle. Don Larreaga was wearing a shirt with a wrinkle in it, and two hours later the wrinkle was gone. In that window of time he must have changed his shirt. His secretary says he didn't change in his office, and his driver says they didn't go home."

"Are you suggesting we investigate where he changed?"

"Well . . . yeah . . ."

"I'll make a note of that. But first I want you to take a look at this video that some tourists sent in last night.

It was unintentionally recorded by the shoe shiner who works the corner down the street. They asked him to take a photo, but he pressed the video button instead. Take a look."

Lupita watched the video of a young couple posing and smiling. After a couple of seconds the woman asked, "Got it? Did it come out okay?"

"I don't know, I guess, here, take a look," answered the shoe shiner.

The phone was still recording, so the couple became blurry as the camera focused on Lupita crossing the street next to an unknown man who was heading in the direction of the delegado's car. Inocencio was already at the door, ready to open it for his boss. The delegado was on his phone but raised his free hand to wave at the strange man, whom Lupita almost ran into. The man waved back, and then the camera jerked toward the sky, ending the video.

"As you can see, the suspect's face isn't clearly visible from this angle. He is our only suspect, and you are our only witness, so we will require you to assist our sketch artist."

"I don't know if I can. I didn't get a good look at him. I mean, I did, but I don't remember his face."

"Please make an effort. Any detail will be of great help and I'm sure your cunning observation skills will come in handy. The artist is waiting for you."

Lupita—for the first time in years—felt appreciated by the man sitting in front of her. It made her feel great. Her mood skyrocketed, and her tongue loosened.

"What I can say right off the bat is that if this man is the killer I don't understand how you think he killed the delegado from that distance. But whatever, if he's the one who did it we're in trouble because that man walks without the slightest hint of fear."

Captain Martinez smiled again. He definitely liked this rough woman.

LUPITA LIKED TO KNIT AND EMBROIDER

Each activity had its own appeal and charm. If Lupita had to choose between them, she would find herself in a great dilemma.

She was passionate about knitting because it allowed her to reach a state of peacefulness, and she loved to embroider because it let her express her creativity. Both activities were liberating. They allowed her to exist outside of time. It was during her prison sentence that she'd learned to knit, and she had discovered that this activity made the hours fly by as she lost her sense of time. When she was able to concentrate on each stitch, every thought that tormented her mind disappeared. There were only courses, wales, and the trail of peace that the synchronized motion of her hands left behind. At the end of the day she had a piece of fabric that she could show her fellow inmates to prove that she had accomplished something good, dignified, and beautiful. Stitch by stitch she recovered her dignity and freedom.

Embroidery also had its charm. She loved to embroider a piece and then apply sequins. One of the things she liked the most about working with sequins was that if she messed up the position of a sequin it was easy to correct the mistake. If the needle had made a wrong turn and the sequin was placed crookedly, all she had to do was thread the needle back through in the opposite direction and that would fix the error. It undid the stitch and the sequin was free to be repositioned correctly.

That afternoon she had been correcting stitch after stitch. Between her injured finger and her hangover you could say she had chosen the worst day for embroidering. To make matters worse, the swollen finger prevented her from wearing a thimble, so she pricked it constantly with the needle. Still, Lupita had no other choice but to embroider against all odds, because she planned on going dancing that night. She needed to feel approval, and she wanted to stand out above everyone on the dance floor. She wanted to shine and laugh. She wanted to shake her hips, delightfully wrapped in her marvelous sequined dress.

As she passed the needle through the fabric she thought about the path of whatever object had slit the delegado's throat wide open. Whatever it was, it pierced his neck side to side. But what could it have been? What could be sharp enough to slice through like that but at the same time leave no trace? She could not believe that the Crime Scene Unit had not found a single shred of evidence. Just as the needle was piercing the fabric, something had pierced Larreaga's neck fast enough to be invisible to the naked eye, and it must have crashed to pieces against something. Her obsessive mind dragged her back to the moment of the crime despite her reluctance. She wanted to forget it all, to think of something else. Most of all, she wanted to celebrate what she considered her final triumph over alcohol. Since the fifth of tequila she had drank before her meeting with Captain Martinez that morning, she had not had another drink. Lupita took that as a sign that she could control her drinking. She powered through the embroidery of the sequined dress, and as she was slipping into it, she heard loud banging on her door and Celia's shrill voice yelling, "GUADALUPEEEEE!!!!"

Celia calling her by her given name instead of the shortened Lupita was a very bad sign. She carefully cracked the door, and Celia shoved her way in.

"What's the matter with you? How could you say that shit about Gomez in front of everyone? My clients expect discretion and anonymity! I told you that in confidence and you pull this bullshit on me?"

"Calm down Celia, let me explain!"

"You have nothing to explain, *pendeja*. I can tell you're drunk again. Fuck you! I thought you were worth something, but I realize you're nothing but a fucking wino that can't wait to pass out in the street."

"Don't speak to me like that."

"I'll speak to you however I please, because it's the last time we'll ever talk! I'll have you know that Gomez sent the legal department after me and they shut down my beauty parlor because of you. Happy now? Go celebrate in your whorish dress!"

Celia stormed out of Lupita's apartment and slammed the door.

Lupita fell back on a chair, stunned and hurt by Celia's words. She had never seen her so enraged. Lupita felt that this breakup with her best friend left her defenseless. Like Celia had let go of her hand and dropped her down a bottomless pit. She had nothing to hold on to, like a sequin that had its thread cut. It was a feeling Lupita had experienced years before, the day she began her prison sentence.

The only thing that had saved her then was knitting. In prison she had become a compulsive knitter. Knitting allowed her to unite, to connect, to integrate. With every stitch she held on to dear life. Threads hold us together. That's why every time she got wasted Lupita asked whomever she was with to hold her hand. She knew that if they let go she'd dissolve, be lost forever in nothingness. She would forget about everything and everyone and lose her mind completely.

When these thoughts overcame her, the only thing that kept her sane was the hope that not all was lost. That everyone could be rescued. In knitting jargon, when a stitch comes loose from the rest it is "dropped," and it leaves a hole in the garment. The wonderful thing is that it can be rescued and reattached with a hook. In real life, when one severs the connections that bind them to the pattern of life it also causes a hole, an enormous one. But that doesn't mean there's no solution. People can be rescued, but they first must recognize the invisible threads that link them to others, our points of union. Our points of contact. That's why Lupita still couldn't fathom why her colleagues—who thought they were hot shit—couldn't investigate criminals' points of contact. That was the key. She didn't just mean linking users to dealers or murderers to accomplices, but discovering those deep threads that people use to knit their personal story, their hidden threads. One thread leads to another, and so forth, but what makes a thread want to become part of a pattern? Finding the answer to those questions was

Lupita's specialty, but not tonight. Tonight she felt her last thread had been severed.

LUPITA LIKED TO DANCE

When she danced she would enter an endless trance in which nothing else mattered. She could dance for hours, and the pain in her feet disappeared completely. Her feet always hurt because when she was a girl she never had a new pair of shoes. She always wore hand-me-downs from the daughters of her mother's employers. Of course, she never got shoes that fit her; some were too large, some were too small. Consequently, her feet were irreparably damaged. But that didn't keep her from going out to a dance hall every weekend.

She liked to know men were staring at her body. It aroused her. She was wearing the little black sequined number she had been repairing a few hours before. It was a vintage dress from the '40s she had bought at the Lagunilla market. Fashion back then was elegant yet appropriate for chubby people like her. The dress draped at the waist and it disguised her belly. She had let her long black hair down and styled it like María Félix in the film *Doña Diabla*. Usually she kept it braided and hidden under her police cap. She looked spectacular. The femme fatale persona suited her.

She had decided to go out in spite of the altercation with Celia because she was sure that dancing would cheer her up. As soon as she sat down she ordered a bottle of rum and some Cokes. It only took half an hour for her to drink it all. She wasn't aware of how dramatically she was relapsing into alcoholism. The only thing that mattered to her now was drinking. Just like before, when her love for booze surpassed her love for anyone or anything. Back when she loved no man, no woman, no dog, no taco or torta. All she cared about was drinking bottle after bottle. The reason was irrelevant, the excuses infinite: someone gave her the stink eye, her mother had died, the government was corrupt, the president was an imbecile. This night it was because Celia was mad at her. Lupita was falling into the same pattern. Even worse, she was getting really pissed off because a lot of people were just sitting at their tables instead of dancing. She was there to have a good time and people were not cooperating. She tried to get their attention, signing and gesturing for them to hit the dance floor, but no one obeyed. Lupita got tired of this, so she found a dance partner who didn't resist. If the rest of the bitter assholes just wanted to sit, so be it! But she wasn't going to let her big night go to waste.

Lupita thought that people who didn't dance were selfish and lonely. Dancing required one to follow a partner and move at their same rhythm. A good dance partner could become one with the other. He or she could feel, predict, and anticipate his or her partner's movements in a game of harmony. But Lupita was also aware that there were men who were bitter and selfish even though they danced. These were the technical dancers, the ones who only cared about showing off. They sought the public's approval before their partner's and executed inconsiderate moves like spinning the woman over and over only because it would look great to spectators. That was precisely the kind of fucker she was dancing with. She was on the verge of puking and the jerk didn't even notice. Even worse, this guy's hands didn't give her the slightest confidence. Lupita felt he wasn't holding her firmly enough, and that at any moment she could spin out of control. She suddenly stopped dancing and wobbled to her table, leaving a very bewildered dance partner behind. Lupita never left a dance unfinished but she couldn't spin anymore. She felt phenomenally nauseous. In order to recover she took a large gulp of her Cuba libre and observed the few couples that were dancing.

Lupita loved to discover details that were unnoticed by most people. She could tell what kind of underwear women were wearing: thong, bikini, granny panties, even if a lady wasn't wearing any underwear. With the men it was more fun. To figure out if a man was wearing boxers, briefs, or nothing at all required a certain degree of audacity, and Lupita had more than enough. From the way he danced Lupita could tell a man who merely fucked from a man who knew how to make love. It was very revealing to observe how a man caressed his partner's back and how he used his hand to spin the woman in one direction or another. It was not a good sign if he pushed her violently. It was fundamental that he keep a rhythm, and terrible if he didn't. That meant he would likely never have a simultaneous orgasm with his lover. Although in the area of sexuality a lot of factors weighed in, like the man's degree of horniness. To determine this Lupita turned to her very particular method of observation that she referred to as three-cushion billiards. It consisted of observing how much a man was attracted to a woman's curves as she walked by him: if he just looked at her tits, or if he also looked her up and down and then turned to see her ass. Lupita could predict the exact time, to the second, that would pass between the first time a man met a woman and when he looked at her ass. Depending on the subtleness or lust he displayed, Lupita could determine if the man was a horny wanker, just slightly aroused, or a degenerate. Based on her judgment she liked to imagine which man she would consider sleeping with. The only men she definitely never would fuck were rich kids and bodyguards. She found no trust in their gaze, if she could even look at their eyes at all, because they usually wore shades, something that caused her great discomfort. She loathed facing a black screen in which she could only see her own reflection staring back at her.

TEZCATLIPOCA'S BLACK MIRROR

In ancient times the original inhabitants of the Valley of Mexico used to make obsidian mirrors. Obsidian was associated with sacrifice, as it was used to fabricate the knives used to slice open the chests of the sacrificed. An obsidian mirror was a magic object that only sorcerers could use. It is said that if you stared into a black mirror you could travel to another time, another place, to the world of the gods and the forebears. The obsidian mirror was the main attribute of the Aztec deity Tezcatlipoca, whose name means "Smoking Mirror." In black mirrors it was possible to find the different manifestations of human nature. You could know a human being's darkest side but also his or her most luminous. The observer and the object coexist. Legend says that once Tezcatlipoca deceived his brother Quetzalcóatl using a black mirror. By looking into the object Quetzalcóatl saw his dark side, his false identity, and betrayed himself. He had to fight the darkness in order to regain his light.

Lupita suddenly noticed that rich kids and their bodyguards had overrun the dance hall. That had to be the reason why no one was dancing. Those fucking brats ruined everything. Why go to a dance hall if you can't even dance? When they discovered a popular spot, they took over and arrived in droves to do as they please. They got wasted and abused the power they had from their fathers' positions and their hired muscle. Lupita, as a general rule, hated bodyguards. The only time she didn't hate them was when they waited outside for their employers. When they were alone they dropped their pretense of toughness and solemnity and relaxed. They joked, talked about sports, and laughed. But as soon as their employers came close, their gazes grew cold and their bodies tense, and their butt cheeks clenched tighter than a delegación's budget during electoral periods.

Lupita observed a rich kid trying to convince a girl to dance with him. The girl was refusing. The rich kid insisted, and the girl's boyfriend defended her. One of the bodyguards stepped in and drew his gun. Lupita reacted with lightning speed. She quickly reached the bodyguard and kicked the gun out of his hand. In the blink of an eye two more bodyguards cornered Lupita, but she held her ground.

"Ooooh, how scary! Look at all the bodyguards. Come at me, c'mon motherfuckers. I'll take you all. You're fucked."

Lupita's attitude threw them off and created enough of a diversion for a large group of security guards from the dance hall to intervene and defuse the conflict. After a heated discussion with some shoving—which ripped Lupita's dress—the security guards bounced the rich kids and their bodyguards before they shot up the place. Lupita followed them to the front door chanting, "Pussies! Pussies!"

She could feel she was being watched. A lot of people were staring at her, some with fear, some with admiration, and one onlooker gave her special attention. It was Captain Martinez, who stared at her fixedly.

Even though Lupita was intrigued to know why the captain was there, she had so much adrenaline pumping through her that she didn't know how to react.

"Why don't you take a picture?"

"Lupita?"

"Yeah!"

"I'm sorry, it's just that I didn't recognize you out of uniform."

"What do you want, Captain?"

"I was looking for you because new evidence came up."

"Who told you I was here?"

"Your neighbor, I believe Celia is her name."

"That fucking bitch!"

"Excuse me?"

"Look, Captain, since you're here, you might as well come dance with me. Then you can talk about whatever you want."

Not one to hesitate, Captain Martinez took Lupita by the hand and led her to the dance floor. Lupita felt like a child protected by her father. His was a big, loving hand. She immediately fantasized about that warm hand running over her entire body.

"I've got good news, Lupita. The sketch you worked on with our artist has been of great help. Licenciado Buenrostro has identified the suspect as one of the street vendors."

"Oh, Captain, why don't you tell me all this stuff later? I really like this song. Let me enjoy it."

The band was playing one of Lupita's favorite songs, "Pedro Navaja" by Rubén Blades. Lupita inched closer to the captain and appreciated how well their bodies fit together. Lupita's breasts rested perfectly on Martinez's belly. It was like he and she had been designed for each other. They were dancing so close that Lupita could feel the captain's breath on her neck. "Life gives you surprises, life gives you surprises" chimed the song's chorus, at the precise moment Lupita noticed the captain wasn't wearing underwear and had an erection. What a surprise indeed! Lupita excitedly pressed her thick curves against the captain. She never imagined that her chubby body could provoke such a fortunate reaction. Her self-esteem took a quantum leap. She felt a knot in her stomach and, much to her dismay, had to excuse herself to run to the bathroom to throw up.

Lupita barely had time to hunch over a sink in the women's room before her stomach emptied itself. Immediately, the attendant—who was none other than the shaman Concepción Ugalde, better known as Conchita—rushed to her aid. She affectionately rubbed Lupita's back while she heaved, and then helped her clean up. Conchita showed no sign of judgment. As a bathroom attendant she had witnessed many similar scenes, but it was still admirable how she tended to Lupita. They were old acquaintances. Lupita had been visiting this dance hall once a week for many years, as many years as Conchita had been the one in charge of preventing the sale and consumption of drugs in the women's bathroom.

"Thanks, Doña Conchita."

"You're welcome child. Do you feel better?"

"Yeah, I think so."

"Good. When did you fall off the wagon?"

"Just recently. Don't worry. It's under control."

"Well, I guess you know all about that."

"I'm just having a real hard time getting over the delegado's death. He died in my arms, you know."

Conchita stopped cleaning, shocked by what she had just heard. "You're the cop that was on the scene?"

"Yeah, didn't you see me all over the news?"

"No, I don't watch TV."

"Good for you."

"Hey, did you happen to see who attacked the delegado?" Conchita asked, getting a bottle of disinfectant to scrub at the sink and anxiously awaiting an answer.

"Guess what, Doña Conchita?" Lupita said, smoothing out her dress. "I just fell in love!"

"You don't say. With who?"

"With an incredible man!"

"Does he drink, too?"

"I don't know, but that's not important."

"If you say so."

"Anyways, I quit drinking. This is just for today."

"So now it turns out that 'just for today' is an excuse to drink? What would the people in your AA group say about that? You're not going anymore, are you?"

"Aw Conchita, don't be like that. We'll talk later, okay? My man is waiting for me."

"Well at least rinse out your mouth before you go." Conchita handed Lupita a small bottle of mouthwash she kept in a drawer, and she noticed Lupita's wounded finger. "What happened to your hand?"

"I got a glass shard stuck in my finger, can you believe that?"

"Glass? But how?"

"I think it's from the delegado's phone."

As Lupita rinsed her mouth, Conchita called someone on her cell phone. She spoke briefly with whoever was on the line. It was inaudible to Lupita due to her loud gargling. Conchita hung up in a hurry.

"Thank you, Doña Conchita. You're the best!"

"You're welcome, child. Have a nice night and remember that if you need help I have a friend who runs a rehab center."

"You don't give up, do you? I told you, I'm not drunk. Well, maybe a little, but don't worry, a bump will fix that! Hahaha."

Conchita did not appreciate Lupita's joke. She nodded her head in disapproval and grasped Lupita by the arm before she walked out the door. She asked Lupita for her number so she could reach her and keep up with her health. Lupita took a pen that was on the counter and started jotting down her phone number directly on Conchita's dress.

"Child, what is wrong with you?"

"Don't get mad, Conchita. This way you won't lose it!"

Conchita once again nodded her head in disapproval. Lupita left the bathroom with a feeling of freshness in her mouth, but she ran straight into a man in the hallway, losing her balance. She turned furiously and was frozen with shock: in front of her stood the very same man who'd crossed the street alongside her the day of the delegado's death. She was dumbstruck. The man was wearing the same ear gauges and labret piercing. After an awkward second, both he and Lupita went their separate ways.

Lupita had three options: go after the man and arrest him, go back to Captain Martinez and tell him about it so he could handle the arrest, or go find some cocaine and enjoy the rest of the night. She chose the last one. She knew exactly where in the dance hall to find the best coke, and she immediately headed in that direction. She was in such a hurry that she didn't see the man she'd run into head into the women's bathroom. He knocked on the door and when Conchita came out they had a suspicious conversation.

LUPITA LIKED TO BE RIGHT

Nothing annoyed her more than being contradicted. She quarreled vehemently, argued endlessly without rhyme or reason, and even mixed up her arguments. In a nutshell: she was very stubborn. Convincing others that she was right was her passion. In her life she had made many mistakes just to prove her point. For example, all her friends had warned her that when he became her boyfriend Manolo was going to put her through a lot of suffering.

She didn't heed their warnings. The man attracted her so much that she overlooked all the telltale signs. She never acknowledged that he was an alcoholic, or how violent he could get when he was drunk. When they got married and the beatings began, Lupita kept quiet. She couldn't stand the thought of her friends saying "we told you so," so she pretended to be in a harmonious relationship just so they wouldn't have the pleasure of being right. It would mean defeat, and she wasn't ready to admit to it. Not until Manolo beat her so badly that she had to go to the hospital did Lupita confess the abuse she had been subjected to. That day she couldn't decide what was worse, the pain in her ribs or her wounded pride.

On this morning she couldn't decide what was worse: her headache, her depression, her uncontrollable desire to sleep, or the anger from hearing terrible comments about Licenciado Larreaga, her dear and admired delegado. Her face was red, and she had an urge to hit someone. And as if her physical and moral hangover weren't enough, she had to sit there and listen to a bunch of assholes talking shit.

So what if Licenciado Larreaga had made political compromises in order to govern? That didn't mean he got dirty money from it! She refused to accept that the delegado had been corrupt. Lupita would stick her neck out for him. She couldn't understand how there could be people mean enough to bad-mouth such an honest man. A deep depression began to overtake her. If anyone had asked about her mood, all she'd be capable of answering would be "shitty." And not just because of the delegado's death. Having slept with Captain Martinez while wasted made her very sad, because for some time now she had been haunted by an absurd thought: she could never know when would be her last time having sex. A woman perfectly remembers her first time, but could never predict when would be her last, and that worried her tremendously. That's why she always tried to enjoy sex to the fullest, and she tried to soak in every detail to keep in her memory just in case there was no next time. For the past few hours she had been trying to remember every kiss and every caress, no matter how insignificant. She had all the time in the world for this. The cocaine she'd inhaled at the dance hall had diminished the effects of the alcohol she drank, but it also kept her up all night. When Captain Martinez left to go to work, she had stayed up waiting for the sun to rise, feeling guilty as hell. As soon as she recalled every instant of the passionate night, her mind began to torment her. Her addiction and lust had prevented her from capturing the delegado's possible murderer. She couldn't stop thinking about how wrong her actions had been. What worried her most was the feeling of losing control once more. The first time she'd felt like this was when she smoked marijuana. Under the influence of weed she heard more than she usually did, and she noticed things she had never seen before. Pot allowed her to overcome the limits imposed by her body, which she liked, but it also altered her sense of space and time. Not controlling her senses and not knowing when the effects would wear off really scared her. And now she felt the same way. The euphoria from the cocaine was gone, leaving a vacuum that was instantly filled with depression. To top it all off, the opinions about the delegado that she was overhearing were terribly disheartening.

Once again, Lupita found herself in the hallway of the Delegación Iztapalapa offices, this time waiting to speak with Buenrostro. After Larreaga's death, Buenrostro had been named interim delegado. There were about a dozen people waiting to see him, and as they waited they all spoke their minds about the current state of affairs. Lupita listened and grew more annoyed. She did not agree with anything she was hearing. She was standing across from Gonzalo Lugo, Mami's right-hand man, who was in the company of several street vendors. There were two young women in the group, and Lupita judged them harshly. If she had to name one thing that annoyed her most, it would probably be the way that girls from the countryside dressed when they came to the city. They immediately got rid of their *huipiles* and threw on a pair of hip-hugger jeans and crop tops that only accentuated their bellies and love handles. When she pictured them dressed in the traditional garments of their indigenous communities, the girls immediately recovered their beauty and dignity. Trading the elegance, originality, and grace of their ancestral clothing for the uniformity of imported, sweatshop clothes designed to give a false sense of status to the wearer made those women usurpers. As she stared them down, Lupita asked herself, *Why do they cut off their braids and get horrible perms like Mami? Why do they dress that way? Why do they try so hard to be something they're not?*

FIVE HUNDRED YEARS EARLIER

The penalty for wearing indigenous clothing was one hundred lashes, a fine of four *reales*, or prison. The Spaniards had banned indigenous clothing because after the conquest they demanded that the natives speak, dress, eat, and act according to the colonizers' commands. Those who obeyed were allowed to dress and decorate themselves in the Spanish tradition as a reward for their submission to the new laws.

Of course, the girls Lupita harshly criticized also had their own opinions about how tight Lupita's uniform and bulletproof vest looked on her. They were even. As they waited to be received by Buenrostro they carried on their conversation, and Lupita had to listen really hard because they were keeping their voices down.

"So what does Mami have to say about this?"

"She's fucking pissed. We're not playing games here. They better not try to say that Larreaga never got his cut."

"But you gave it to him directly, right?"

"Of course, bitch. All cash, in a shoebox, like always!"

Lupita felt a lump in her throat. She refused to believe what she was hearing. A wave of indignation drove her to interject on the delegado's behalf.

"Hey, could you please mind your words? Don Larreaga's body hasn't even left the morgue and you're already slandering him? Have a little respect, will you?"

"Well, with all due respect, mind your own business you third-rate pisser."

"Your grandma's the pisser, asshole!"

"She may be a pisser but she's not corrupt like your delegado."

"The corrupt one is Mami!"

"Are you sure she's corrupt?"

"Yes."

"Then why don't you report her?"

"Because I'm not stupid. It wouldn't accomplish anything! Don't be an imbecile."

Suddenly everyone fell quiet. Selene, the delegado's widow, entered the hallway escorted by Inocencio. The street vendors all stood up and hypocritically offered their condolences. Selene thanked them with a slight nod. She was dressed in black and kept her sunglasses on. Inocencio was carrying a box in which Lupita assumed were some of the delegado's personal effects. On her way out, Selene noticed Lupita and walked toward her.

"Good morning."

"Good morning, ma'am. I'm very sorry for your loss."

"Thank you. I wanted to tell you that I appreciate you staying with my husband until the ambulance arrived."

"It was my duty."

"Listen, I was told that you picked up his phone?"

"Yes ma'am, but I delivered it to my superiors."

"Ah! Well, thank you for everything."

"At least your husband told you he loved you before he died."

"Excuse me?"

"Over the phone, didn't you hear him?"

Selene raised her sunglasses for a second and looked at Lupita with tremendous pain spreading across her face. Lupita knew instantly that the delegado had cheated on his wife. It took just one glance to prove it. The look in Selene's eyes was the same she saw in her mother's eyes when Trini learned that her husband—Lupita's stepfather—had molested her daughter. It was the same look she saw in her own eyes when she looked in a bathroom mirror after catching her husband Manolo petting her goddaughter's pubescent chest at a quinceañera party. The girl was barely eleven years old, but two small mounds were beginning to show. Manolo—completely drunk—had grabbed her from behind and was rubbing her still forming breasts with a disgusting lust. When Manolo realized he had been caught, he shoved the girl aside and she ran in terror to the other side of the patio. A wave of nausea made Lupita seek refuge in a bathroom, and that was when she saw that look of pain in her own face.

"Excuse me, where's the restroom?" said Selene.

"This way, ma'am. Let me walk you," Lupita said to the widow.

"Don't worry," Inocencio said. "I'll take her. Thank you."

Lupita watched them walk away with tears in her eyes. In that moment Larreaga came crashing down from the pedestal upon which Lupita had placed him. All evidence pointed to him being a cheating husband. What if the delegado had not only cheated on his wife but also committed acts of corruption? That would mean Lupita was wrong. That she wasn't always right. That she catalogued people according to her own longing instead of reality, and that hurt like hell. Fuck, it hurt! Now Lupita couldn't rely on her own judgment, which meant she couldn't even trust herself. She, who had relapsed into alcohol and drugs despite having vowed at her son's grave to never do it again. If she couldn't trust her own word, what hope was left in the world?

Buenrostro's secretary yanked her out of her moping. She called Lupita by name and asked her to proceed to the director's office.

"Good morning, Lupita. Please take a seat."

"Thank you, Licenciado."

"Listen, I received a copy of the suspect sketch based on your statement, and it seems to be a street vendor. He has a booth in the park where he sells obsidian artifacts. Are you sure he had those gauges in his ears and the labret piercing?"

"Labret?"

"Yeah, it's a piercing below the lower lip, usually the jewelry is a pointy shaft instead of a ring."

"Yeah, he did."

Lupita debated whether to tell Buenrostro that she'd run into the guy at the dance hall. She decided against it because confessing would prove her the worst cop in the world.

"That will be all. Thank you very much. I'm not trying to get rid of you, but I do have a lot of other people to meet with."

Lupita left the office, and on her way to the building's exit she saw Don Carlos—her AA sponsor. She turned around and headed for a door at the back of the building marked for authorized personnel only. She walked as fast as she could, trying to blend in with the crowd. She couldn't face her sponsor with alcohol on her breath. Life is ironic: two days ago she would have given anything to talk to him, but now it was pointless.

Carlos had been searching for Lupita for hours. He had read about her in the newspapers and wanted to offer his support. What worried him the most was knowing that Lupita had reached out to him and he hadn't been available to help. He had been mugged a few days back and his cell phone had been stolen. That was why Lupita couldn't reach him. Carlos knew the impact this kind of event could have on the soul of an emotional cripple, and he wanted to help ease Lupita's pain as much as he could.

LUPITA LIKED TO OBSERVE THE SKY

To carefully contemplate the trajectory of celestial bodies. To reflect on how a planet hides behind another during its orbit. Since her son's death, when she spent the night observing how her own shadow was projected on the child's face, eclipses had fascinated her. It was quite astounding to bear witness to the disappearance of a heavenly body and its subsequent reappearance in the firmament. If one can no longer see something, or someone, that doesn't necessarily mean that the object has disappeared completely. Sometimes one is, and sometimes one isn't. To Lupita it was a phenomenon not unlike being drunk. Those who have seen the eyes of a drunk understand this well. In the depths of those eyes another person appears, and disappears when they sober up.

Returning to her body after a binge was very irritating. The discomfort experienced during a hangover was infernal, and yet Lupita—for some unknown reason—enjoyed it. She accepted it as part of the recovery process. She saw it as a sort of rebirth.

LIGHT VS. DARKNESS

The creation of the sun by the hands of the gods was crucial to the birth and support of life. In antiquity it was believed that every day a battle between light and darkness took place in the sky. If the dark night were to triumph, humanity's existence would be endangered. All living beings, as an active part of the Universe, had to recognize the movements of the heavens within their own bodies and become warriors of the light in the battle to defeat the dark. If the light were victorious in their internal struggle, the sun would be restored, because the fight between opposing forces in the sky was something that happened inside and out, above and below. Those who observed the movements in the sky and acknowledged they were part of the heavens became gods, became the reborn sun.

Every time Lupita got wasted part of her would disappear, and when Lupita was absent from herself she didn't know where she was. There had to be a place where she existed while the alcohol wore off, but where was this? Were there two Lupitas? A sober Lupita and a drunk Lupita? In that case there had to be two minds: a sane mind and a demented mind that governed their respective Lupita. Could it be said that the sane mind sat on the bench resting while the other mind got drunk? Was that the reason why, upon sobering up, the sane mind had no memory of what the demented mind had ordered? Lupita didn't know, but she was hopeful knowing that a part of her remained intact, unaware of the excesses in which her out-of-control body indulged. There was a Lupita who remained innocent and pure, a Lupita who wanted to be welcomed back into the world instead of being berated for drinking too much.

Lupita opened her eyes slowly and was surprised to see thousands of stars looking back. For an instant that heavenly spectacle took away her breath, but then a wave of pain washed over her entire body. The pain was so strong that she regretted coming back from wherever she had been. She felt the chill of early morning. She didn't know where she was. The last thing she remembered was leaving the last of several cantinas she had visited, and stumbling upon a police operation clearing all the street vendors from Cuihtláhuac Park. Apparently the chief of police had ordered the arrest of the suspect based on the sketch from Lupita's description of the suspect. In truth, the delegación authorities were using Lupita's statement as an excuse to finally clear out the park so that the Passion procession would seem better organized and more flashy. The vendors, headed by Mami, had fought back violently against the police.

Earlier that day Lupita, instead of doing the Seven Churches Visitation, had taken a "seven cantinas tour" to ask the Crucified Christ to help her control her drinking. It sounds ridiculous, but it made sense to her at the time. Lupita had walked out of the seventh cantina and was on her way to the police station when she ran into the street vendors. She remembered facing Mami and shooting her a challenging look. But Lupita remembered nothing after that. Now here she was, beat up and lying in the middle of a field.

The blackout obscured everything that had happened between Lupita and Mami. It would take years for Lupita to remember that she had insulted and threatened Mami in front of everyone.

"Fucking Mami *culera*! You're fucked now."

"Are you talking to me, pendeja?"

"Yeah, or do you see any other Mami culera around here? Another thieving, corrupt, drug-pushing whore of a Mami?"

"You're crossing the line, you fucking *naca*. It's bad enough that you're trying to pin the murder on one of my people, so shut your mouth and stop saying shit you can't prove."

"I can prove it all! You know what? I have proof in my phone that you run all the drug trade in Iztapalapa. What do you have to say about that, pendeja?"

Mami had answered with a punch that knocked Lupita to the floor, and she followed up with a few good kicks. At that point a melee ensued between street vendors and the police. Amid the chaos and the screaming no one noticed when Mami took an obsidian knife to the neck and started to bleed out. An ambulance rushed her to the hospital and someone dragged out Lupita and dumped her wherever the hell she was now.

The silence was absolute. The only sounds were the chirping of crickets and cicadas. Lupita tried to get up but fell under her own weight. She tried to figure out where she was and failed at that as well, foiled by darkness. She searched for her phone in her bra. She always kept it there because she had been the victim of pickpockets in the subway before, and her huge tits hid it completely. Fortunately the phone was still on. She dialed Celia's number. No one else came to mind.

"Lupita?"

"Yes."

"Goddammit you scared the shit out of me!"

"Why?"

"Because no one has heard from you. Where are you?"

"I don't know. It's really dark."

"Well, the sun will be out soon. Wait there and see if you recognize anything."

Lupita was very moved by Celia's reaction. She sounded very worried. Apparently she had gotten over her anger because she talked to Lupita like nothing had happened. What Lupita didn't know was that Celia's change in attitude was only because she had seen a news segment about the altercation between the police and the vendors, and caught a glimpse of Lupita being slammed over the head with a two-by-four by the guy who would play Dimas during the Passion procession. After she was struck, someone dragged the passed-out Lupita off screen, and that was the last Celia knew of her friend. Later in the evening Celia's son Miguel had stopped by to visit and made her even more worried. Miguel was a waiter who worked for a catering service. The previous night Mami had hosted a party at her house and the catering service assigned Miguel to work the event. Waiters usually enjoy a certain degree of invisibility. They tend to be ignored, so they overhear all sorts of conversations and confidential information when they're on the job. Mami had been hosting a dinner in honor of Hilario Gomez, who had just announced his intentions to run for delegado. This was Mami's way of very publicly backing him.

At one point during the night Miguel overheard Mami and Gomez talking about recent affairs: "Listen Licenciado, I'm going to need you to help me out with

my vendors. That sketch based on the cop's statement—
Lupita I think her name is—has already affected me
enough. You know how Buenrostro is trying to use that
as an excuse to kick us out of the park, right before the
Passion. It's when our sales are the highest. It's not fair."

"Don't worry. I'll make a note of it."

"I'm really counting on you for this. Maybe you can
give that bitch cop a slap on the wrist so she learns some
manners."

"Again I tell you: don't worry about it. We're here to
help."

As Lupita lay face up on the dirt she remained in
awe of the night sky even though her physical discomfort
made her want to repent for all her sins. What could she
have done to deserve this? Or better still, what had she
not done? If she hadn't gotten completely wasted the previous day she wouldn't have overlooked all the obvious
warning signs that pointed to an oncoming tragedy. Her
mother had taught her to look out for them since she was
little. Lupita knew that when the fire on the stove flickers,
disgrace was looming. How could she not have noticed
the fire fluttering when she heated her coffee pot that

morning? She felt a line of ants pattering along her hand. That meant she was outside the city, and the ants' hurried pace announced the coming of a storm. As if things couldn't get worse! She tried to get up to vomit but one of her legs gave out and she fell. Her leg was surely broken, and from the pain in her side, probably a rib or two as well. Lupita tried to get back on her knees and her hand touched what seemed to be a body lying next to her. She was no longer able to contain her nausea and she vomited with great pain. When the heaving stopped she fell back on the dirt, invaded by terrible fear. If she was lying next to a dead body it was because they had been disposed of together, and she was presumed dead. That meant her "rebirth" would present a threat to someone. When one person becomes a nuisance to another, it's not uncommon for one of the parties to think, *Why doesn't this asshole just die already?* Lupita had thought that many times. First about her stepfather. Then about her husband. Then about Mami. It was useless to dwell on it. The point was someone wanted her dead and thought they had accomplished it. Why? What threat did she pose? What could she get in the way of? Who would benefit from her death?

It had to somehow involve the delegado's murder. Other than that, she had no clue. Well, if she were to be honest, Hilario Gomez was probably still furious about Lupita airing out his secrets in front of everyone. She still didn't think it was that big of a deal. What threat could she pose to him now that everyone knew he regularly got his back waxed?

TEZCATLIPOCA VS. QUETZALCÓATL

The gods Tezcatlipoca ("Smoking Mirror") along with his brother Quetzalcóatl ("Feathered Serpent") were two of the most important deities in the Aztecs' creation myths. Tezcatlipoca harbored a rivalry with his brother Quetzalcóatl over important differences in philosophy. Quetzalcóatl was opposed to human sacrifice, and Tezcatlipoca believed that it was necessary to sustain the sun and therefore life. One time, Tezcatlipoca disguised himself as an old man and offered his brother *pulque*, the sacred drink. Quetzalcóatl took the bait and got drunk. In that altered state he broke all the laws he had set for his people, and even fornicated with his own sister. Shamed by his actions he exiled himself from the city he had founded. He walked east, toward the rising sun. When he reached the ocean he embarked on a vessel and sailed until he reached the sun in the horizon. There, where the sky meets the water, he fused with the sun, recovered his light, and became Venus, the Morning Star: he who makes a path for the sun to be reborn from the dark every day. After the conquest, friars decorated all figures of Quetzalcóatl with Christian symbols.

Lupita didn't notice when she stopped being alone, or how she could see clearly in absolute darkness, but she found herself in the presence of several warriors belonging to the native culture of Iztapalapa. They were dressed in animal skins and wore headdresses ornamented with regal feathers. One of them held an ornate staff and stared deeply at Lupita. They were all sad and angry. For a second she thought she might be hallucinating. Not even under the effects of peyote had she ever had such a clear vision. None of the warriors could speak because their lips were held shut by cactus thorns but Lupita could feel their words inside her head. The warriors said they were very angry. They had been ordered to surrender to the Spaniards and they had obeyed. They were told that these intruders were representatives of the god Quetzalcóatl. They never agreed with the emperor Moctezuma, but they respected his wishes. Now their grieving souls roamed aimlessly because they were unable to defend their children, their women, and their race. They knew that Cortés and his soldiers would never understand their culture so they sealed their lips to ensure that none of their people's secrets and wisdom would ever escape them. They chose eternal silence. Lupita heard the faint sound of war drums beating in unison, rising in volume. She felt that her temples would burst from the pounding. Her entire body began to pulsate to the beat. She heard chanting in Náhuatl and many voices saying, "It's time to speak, it's time to heal. Listen to our tongue, the words of our ancestors are vessels that contain the knowledge of the sky, they are plants that heal the soul. Heed them. Let the sun into your heart, the sun shall once more be reborn for everyone and you must be there to help. The crystal chose you. Don't be afraid, the toad will guide you."

Lupita shut her eyes tight and covered her ears. Fuck! What drug had she taken? She thought she was losing her mind. She had heard legends before, of people seeing the spirits of ancient warriors at a place in Iztapalapa, but she never believed them. Yet there she was, seeing, hearing, her heart racing.

Fortunately, the first rays of sunlight began to cast light on her surroundings and Lupita slowly returned to reality. The native chanting slowly faded into a church choir that sang a poem by Saint Theresa: "The soul is made of crystal, a luminous castle, an oriental pearl, a royal palace with immense chambers to inhabit." Lupita got her breathing under control and tried to focus her vision. The voices went away. The early morning sun was very powerful. Lupita would have given anything for a pair of sunglasses. Her tremendous hangover prevented her from adapting to the sunlight. Through squinted eyes Lupita observed the landscape. She was in the middle of an open field near Eagle's Cave, a cavern near the top of Star Hill. She immediately sent Celia her location.

As she waited for her friend, she observed the man that lay next to her and immediately understood why someone wanted her dead. The body's features matched the description she had given of the man suspected of murdering the delegado. Her colleagues surely planned on "solving" the murder with the discovery of this man's body, along with Lupita's. They would explain it as revenge between drug mafias and would very likely portray Lupita as a crooked cop who was involved. The judicial power always found someone to pay for a crime but wasn't interested in finding the actual perpetrator. In order to pull this off they resorted to sublimely imaginative solutions.

If years before they had been able to assure the population that the murder of a presidential candidate had been the work of a lone gunman even though the victim received more than two gunshots of different calibers and from different directions, this cover-up was a piece of cake!

Celia, who arrived to retrieve Lupita in the middle of a heavy rainfall, confirmed all of her suspicions. She immediately got Lupita up to speed as she and Miguel lifted her into the backseat of the car. Celia spared no detail in explaining how Mami received the same wound as the delegado. Things were getting murky. The media was now pointing at Lupita as the author of both crimes, because she was the only person who could be placed at both scenes, the first resulting in murder and the second leaving Mami on the brink of death. A warrant had been put out for Lupita's arrest.

"What do we do now, mana? You need to be seen by a doctor. Where do you want us to take you?"

"We can't go to a hospital. Take me to an AA center. My identity will be kept secret there."

"Yeah and you could use some time . . ."

"Stop Celia, I can't take your sermons right now and I swear by this," Lupita said, forming a cross with her fingers. "I want to get better without you being on my ass about it."

"Okay, okay, okay. Fine. Just lay back and try to rest."

Celia started the car and began the drive back. On the road they passed Hilario Gomez's car. The former chief advisor was accompanied by a distinguished group of corrupt reporters who would very likely break the news of the discovery of the bodies linked to the delegado's murder. Both Celia and Gomez pretended to not see each other. Neither one waved to the other. Celia had not forgiven her salon being shut down, and Hilario had not forgiven Celia for revealing his personal hygiene secrets.

When Hilario arrived at the place where both bodies had been dumped and found only one, he immediately suspected Celia. A dead woman doesn't just get up and leave by herself.

On the other hand, it was clear to Celia that Hilario had been involved in the death of the man who was lying next to Lupita, as well as the aggression toward her friend.

LUPITA LIKED SOLITUDE AND SILENCE

It took her years to accept it but she really liked to be alone with her thoughts. The day she had begun her prison sentence for killing her son, the world of sounds familiar to her stayed outside the gates. A dense fog of silent fear invaded her ears. It was a fear that chilled to her core, a fear that gave her an itch in her urethra, a fear that crushed her chest. And now, after being dropped off by Celia at the rehab facility, Lupita felt the same way. The dry sound of the door closing behind her announced the arrival of silence. From her own experience she knew that when the voices of parents, the laughter of children, and the whispers of lovers are silenced by the walls of institutions, one's ears immediately search for new vibrations in the air and tune in to new sounds. In stillness one can discover that silence is not silence, and that sound—as a vibration—travels, flies, crosses walls, flows through fences, expands like the beating of a heart, like a constant and ever present pulse.

It had taken Lupita many years of imprisonment to discover that she could hear better in silence, and that she was in better company when she was alone. One is never truly alone, even when our only company is our thoughts, because what are thoughts if not the memory of interactions with others? In silence, Lupita reconnected with the most important people in her life. She carefully took the loose threads of her soul and knit them back together with her loved ones', so they would never be separated again. She connected with a forgotten pulse, with a primal rhythm. It was in prison where Lupita first heard her heartbeat. During her sleepless nights she had even counted how many times her heart beat between sunset and sunrise, experiencing the passing of time within herself.

Now once more she needed time to herself. Quiet. Silence. To recover the Lupita that once was, the Lupita she couldn't even remember anymore. Sometimes she felt like a piece of luggage left behind at an airport, a suitcase full of surprises that no one could see in plain sight. A suitcase that had inside it an entire life's history but would go by unnoticed if its owner—who held the key to its secrets—never found it. She was both the suitcase and the owner. She had to bring these dual aspects of herself together in order to emerge from darkness. And she needed to breathe. Breathe. Breathe.

How it hurt to breathe! After a set of X-rays, the admitting doctor confirmed that she had a broken rib. The worst thing was that nothing could be done about it except to bandage her torso and wait for it to heal. As for her broken femur, that was another story. Her leg had been put in a hard cast that forced her to stay in bed. As for healing the fractures of her soul, those required a different medicine. Lupita knew it, and she was determined to be sober once more. Recapitulation and restructuring required peace, and the tranquilizer she was being given facilitated her rest and silence.

Celia would have killed for five minutes of rest. As soon as she filled out the paperwork for Lupita and said good-bye, she went home to take a shower. She immediately headed to the house of the actress who would portray Mary in the procession. After doing her makeup, she also had to apply makeup on Pontius Pilate and many others. There was a small window of time between Mary and Pontius Pilate, and Celia used it to call Captain Martinez to let him know that Lupita wasn't missing or a fugitive, but was in fact checked into a rehab clinic and urgently needed to talk to him.

Celia then ran to Judas's house and on her way became aware of a great commotion in the delegación. The neighbor who was to portray Judas, and who had been on the waiting list for thirteen years, had been found dead in a field near one of the caves atop Star Hill. Notwithstanding the gravity of the case, the understudy for the part felt completely unprepared to take on the role. Carlos, the murdered Judas, had undergone psychoanalysis for over a year in order to build up his self-esteem. During the Passion procession, the crowds usually assaulted Judas verbally. They would yell horrible things at him as he passed, and the actor had to be capable of keeping his personal identity separate from his character.

Celia was taken aback by the news. The Judas who had been murdered was the same man who had been lying next to Lupita near the cave when she and Miguel picked her up. Celia hadn't paid much attention. She had been focused on helping her friend so she'd disregarded the corpse. Celia had met Carlos. One day before she had done a makeup test and then had walked with him to a dress rehearsal where a group of neighbors were waiting to see if the harness that would hold him after he hung himself from the tree was fitted properly, as it would have to hold him for several hours. Celia wanted to make sure that the makeup she had applied would hold out in the heat. Now she had to repeat the test with Don Neto, the understudy. He'd been waiting for her and was really nervous. Don Neto was a few pounds heavier than the last Judas and prayed the harness would hold him. Never before in all the years of the Passion procession had anything of this sort happened. Everybody was surprised and on edge, Celia most of all, but her professionalism shone through and she performed her duty in a timely manner. She was dying to speak to Captain Martinez again, but it had to be in person. The information she had to share with him was very delicate. In the meantime, between applying eye shadow and mascara, fake eyelashes and fingernails, Celia used every available second to continue her own investigation. She found out that Mami was recovering at the hospital, that Ostión had gone to visit her, and that Hilario Gomez had sent her a phenomenal bouquet wishing her a speedy recovery. She also heard that Mami had reached an agreement with Licenciado Larreaga before his death in which she and her street vendors would evacuate Cuihtláhuac Park, and in exchange the delegación would build them a new shopping plaza where they could sell their products. The person in charge of assigning booths at this new plaza would, of course, be Mami. The ideal grounds for building this project had been a cause for quarrel because a group of traditionalists claimed ownership over the land.

This group had backed Larreaga during his candidacy. Celia was told that Conchita Ugalde—the leader of this group—had organized a breakfast banquet for Larreaga after his triumph, during which she spoke for all traditionalist groups and told the newly elected delegado: "We offer our word and our commitment. In exchange we ask that you not betray us. These lands are sacred to my people. Let us continue to make use of them as our ancestors have, and continue with our traditions. That is all we ask of you." The delegado, with tears in his eyes, said that yes, he would of course respect the lands and uphold this vow. Unfortunately—or at least so Celia heard—he no sooner wiped away his tears than he betrayed those people. With great diligence he expropriated the nine-acre property from the guardians of tradition and offered it to Mami, to whom he owed his position. Without her help he would have never won the election, even if he counted on the votes from the guardians of tradition. Mami had many more people on her payroll. All things considered, Mami's support was worth more than that of the guardians so without further thought the delegado ordered them to evacuate their ancestors' lands. Obviously the guardians were quite upset and refused. One night, approximately a hundred mercenaries tried to evict them forcefully, and the guardians fought back with sticks, stones, and a bullet or two. Police in riot gear had to intervene to restore order.

All of this information came from Don Lupe, a car washer who worked for the delegación. From the curb where he operated he overheard all sorts of conversations and observed the comings and goings of government employees. Don Lupe was going to portray Dimas in the Passion and needed Celia to attach his wig. He was very proud to finally participate in the procession. While Celia attached the wig, she noticed his hand was bandaged.

"What happened to your hand?"

"Oh, it's just a splinter."

"Seems like a big wound."

"Yes ma'am, and I don't even know where it came from. I had just washed the delegado's car, and I'd left my bucket and rag next to where he was murdered."

Celia's detective instinct kicked in.

"And after the whole ordeal was over, I wrung my rag and that's when I got the splinter."

"Was it glass?"

"Yeah! How did you know?"

"Lucky guess. Did you check the bucket for other glass shards?"

"No ma'am, I didn't think to do so. I just threw out the water and tried to bandage my finger because it was bleeding heavily. You don't know how hard it was to get it out. My wife helped me and we had to borrow a magnifying glass from a neighbor because it kept breaking when we tried to pull it."

Celia felt that she had stumbled upon a very important clue and was dying to tell Lupita, but she was so busy that it would have to wait until the next day. What Celia didn't realize, however, was that Gomez's employees had been following her around.

As Lupita lay in bed at the rehab center, oblivious to everything that was happening, she tried to rest and familiarize herself with the new sounds that surrounded her, and which sometimes unexpectedly startled her. She still was not used to the noises from the kitchen, the nurses' conversations, and doors opening and closing. Out of nowhere, and without any context, she began to sing "Canción Mixteca" to herself. She never knew why, but that song always moved her to tears. An enormous sadness overcame her and every time she got drunk she would belt out the lyrics:

> *I'm so far from the land where I was born,*
> *A great nostalgia invades my thoughts.*
> *And being so alone and sad like a leaf in*
> *the wind,*
> *I want to cry, I want to die of grief.*
> *Oh, land of the sun! I long to see you*
> *Now that I am far without light, without*
> *love.*
> *And being so alone and sad like a leaf in*
> *the wind*
> *I want to cry, I want to die of grief.*

Just thinking about the song made Lupita's eyes water. Thinking about the land of the sun, visiting that paradise where nothing was needed, made her so nostalgic! Lupita would have liked to go there without having to die. She would love to enter and exit her body at will without losing consciousness.

HALLUCINOGENIC PLANTS IN THE PRE-HISPANIC WORLD

The use of psychoactive plants in the sacred rituals performed by Mesoamerican Indians was very common, with ancient roots. They were used to induce trances that connected the participants of the ceremony with the god that inhabits everyone. That is why they are referred to as entheogenic. They were used by shamans to cure disease or to delve into their divination practice. Some of these plants are referred to as "medicine." In his *General History of the Things of New Spain*, Friar Bernardino de Sahagún identified various psychoactive plants. Some are still used today by various ethnic groups. One of the most common is peyote. Other plants that have psychoactive substances, or are considered sacred and medicinal, are tobacco flowers (*Nicotiana tabacum*), cocoa flowers (*Quararibea funeris*), thorn apple (*Datura innoxia*), morning glory (*Turbina corymbosa*), and certain fungi known as *teonanácatl.* All of them provoke different reactions: hallucination, trance, or delusion. The presence of shamans during their use guaranteed that participants could "travel" to another reality and return to their bodies safe and sound. The experience of the trip allowed "patients" to reflect upon the cause of their disease and how to recover their health, gave them a sense of well-being, and, most importantly, reminded them of the divinity that dwelled within them.

Leaving her body unconsciously was not all that pleasant. Lupita would never forget the shock on the day she had woken up next to an unknown man, and not just any man, a significantly repulsive one. After observing him with disgust for a moment she inspected the bed to measure the extent of the damages. What she discovered was even more horrifying: the sheets were covered in all sorts of fluids and stains. On the positive side, she went to rehab straight after that. On the negative side, as soon as she got out she relapsed very quickly. It wasn't until her son's death that she was able to evade the bottle for several years.

Now she had relapsed and found herself in a similar situation, except this time she had woken up next to a cadaver. She didn't want to risk a next time. She wished with all her soul to live sober and conscious of her actions.

LUPITA LIKED TO RUN

Until she collapsed, until she couldn't feel the pain in her legs anymore, until she transcended all bodily sensations and entered a trancelike state. When she was young she tried to go for a run every weekend, but for some time now her work had gotten in the way. Running had always been a way to escape. It permitted her to flee from reality in a healthier way than alcohol did. When she drank she lost control over her mind and body, but when she ran she recovered it. Running gave her a complete sense of freedom, and that was why she felt so uncomfortable being a prisoner, limited in her movement. She had an IV in her left hand, and she was getting tired of it. When she first checked in she was grateful for every drop of saline solution that went into her bloodstream, but now that she felt significantly better, the artificial umbilical cord gave her mixed feelings. On one hand she liked knowing that her body received all the nutrients it needed from a single source. It was nice to travel back to the time when her mother provided sustenance through a cord that joined their bodies. But on the other hand her condition forced her to stay still if she wanted to stay connected to the cord that nourished her. She couldn't move her arm at will. She couldn't wander like she wanted to. She had to stay connected to the IV—sleep with it, bathe with it.

To make matters worse the cast on her leg impeded her movement even more. Lupita felt restless on the bed. Her body screamed out to change position, but she couldn't obey. She felt like a prisoner again, but this time to her own physical condition. The worst part was that she had brought this upon herself. Nobody forced her at knifepoint to go to the cantinas. Nobody forced her to violently insult everyone within her reach. Nobody twisted her arm to do so much cocaine. These had all been her choices. Was her current condition caused by an unresolved emotional illness? Maybe so, but no matter the reason only she could decide how to face her problems. If people were to write about her they could credibly refer to a "lone killer": Lupita, the one responsible for everything. Coincidentally, that was what the people in charge of the delegado's murder investigation were trying to do. That morning's newspaper contained a front-page article that gave a new version of the facts. According to the paper, the delegado had committed suicide with a box cutter he had hidden in his shirtsleeve. Where was this box cutter? No one knew. And where was the suicide note? No one knew. Why did he kill himself? No one knew. None of that was important. The priority was to close the case, get on with the Passion procession, and make sure it went off without a hitch. Everything seemed to be going according to plan.

Newscasts were covering the procession step by step. As Judas, Don Neto was doing a fine job of resisting the insults hurled at him by the crowds. There was only one instance in which he wanted to respond to an aggression, but vanity held him back. If he got in a fistfight with the Nazarene who insulted him, the wig that Celia placed on his head could fly off and his baldness would be exposed to everyone.

The only good thing that came from the Passion procession was that due to the tremendous need to carry on with it, Lupita was no longer a murder suspect. That put her in a more comfortable position but there was still a distinct possibility that the people who had left her for dead would find out she was alive and would come looking for her.

Maybe it was from all the saline solution, or because she remembered the murder, but Lupita suddenly had an irresistible urge to urinate. She called out to a nurse for help but got no answer. With great effort she stood up and limped to the bathroom while dragging along the IV stand. Outside, fireworks were going off constantly. The Passion procession was at its peak. Every loud boom reverberated in Lupita's head. The noise annoyed her, but her need to pee was stronger.

As soon as she got to the bathroom and sat down, peeing brought her enormous pleasure. She was so relieved that she didn't notice the loud fireworks fading into rapid gunfire, until she heard people running and screaming down the hall. Lupita instinctively got up and hid behind the bathroom door. The door to her room was kicked open and several bullets hit her empty bed. It took a few seconds before she heard anything else. She carefully peered out from behind the door, just able to see the bed in her room. The covers were in a bunch so it looked like she was underneath them. A man walked to the bed and swiftly raised the covers. Lupita leaned back against the wall and held her crutch like a weapon. An absurd thought crossed her mind: *Shit, at least I was able to pee this time!* Someone kicked the bathroom door open, and Lupita held her breath. She heard more yelling and people running down the hallway. Someone had ordered a retreat. More gunfire and shouting made the attacker leave her room. Lupita leaned on the IV stand and knew that she had to run. She didn't know where she got the strength to step out into the hall and leave the rehab center, much less how she wasn't shot. Adrenaline pushed her to run, but her legs weren't responding.

A block from the rehab facility she ran into a group of Nazarenes at the head of the procession. They were approaching the base of Star Hill, where the celebration would culminate with the crucifixion of Christ. Lupita had never been a big fan of the Passion. She respected it as part of tradition but nothing more. But now it took on a whole new meaning for her. She joined the procession because she had no other choice. Everyone was dressed in long tunics and didn't seem to mind that she was only wearing a hospital gown. They may have thought that it was a new way to participate in the procession and that her IV stand was just another cross to bear. Lupita was trying to remove the needle from her hand, but it was hard for her to keep her balance on one leg while trying to rip off the adhesive gauze. When she finally got the needle out, she collapsed on the ground. The pain in her leg was intense. People walked by her and paid no attention. Everybody was concentrated on their own thing, praying and supplicating themselves to Christ on the cross.

Lupita observed these people and wished she shared their faith. She had lost hers at a very young age, the very day she was raped by her stepfather. Where was God that morning? Why had He allowed that? She had not forgiven Him since then and had veered away from religion completely. One of the requisites to join AA was to surrender to a higher power. Lupita did this but never in a religious sense. Honestly, she hadn't ever surrendered to a superior power because she couldn't even grasp the concept. Nonetheless, after removing the IV needle she felt an urge to connect to something else, something immaterial that could keep her alive. As a child she had heard that the center of the cross is where the four winds meet and where the spirit of existence resides. Lupita liked to think that Christ had felt no pain on the cross because when He was nailed to the wood His soul migrated to the center of the cross. That place outside of time where people who left their body went. It was the place she so eagerly sought to reach through alcohol, the place where suffering did not exist. Physical pain definitely encouraged the elevation of the spirit. Her body, tired of suffering, wanted to leave aside all of its ailments and rest.

Lupita rested her head between her knees and gave up. She asked whichever superior force would listen to be allowed to rest in the center. In the spirit, where there is peace. Where there is light. Light. Light.

STAR HILL

At the top of Star Hill—called Huizachtépetl by the Aztecs—was where light was sought, where light was yearned for, where light was venerated since pre-Hispanic times by means of the Ceremony of the New Fire. The hill is 8,070 feet above sea level, and from the top you can see the entire Valley of Mexico. Lighting the New Fire marked the end of a solar cycle and the beginning of a new one. The ceremony called for human sacrifice.

The Nazarenes came to a halt. The time for crucifixion had come. The atmosphere at Star Hill was magnificent and poignant. All the attendants kept completely quiet as Christ died on the cross. Everyone who had carried a cross raised it in unison. Lupita closed her eyes and allowed herself to be invaded by the faith that surrounded her. Absolute peace engulfed her. Clarity took over her mind and comforted her. If she were to die then, she would die in peace. If a bullet found her, so be it! She didn't know why, but for the first time in her life she was sure that death didn't exist. Rather, everything converged in the center of the Universe, everything came together. Everything took shape over and over in an eternal and continuous cycle.

Lupita left the world for a moment. She didn't hear sirens approaching the rehab facility. She didn't see gunmen run past her. The only thing she was sure of was that an invisible thread had emerged from her heart and had risen to the sky where it connected with the heart of the heavens. It was so powerful that everything happening around her faded into the background. She didn't notice a gunman stop in front of her and shoot, and she didn't realize that the IV stand saved her life when it blocked the bullet. She did hear the gun being fired, however. Alarmed, she opened her eyes and saw Tenoch—a man with ear gauges and a labret piercing—pull her away from her attacker's aggression. He took her in his arms and led her away from the scene, which rapidly evolved into chaos.

Lupita offered no resistance and meekly let Tenoch guide her. This man was the only person she could trust.

LUPITA LIKED TO SOW

To touch the earth. To walk barefoot on it. To water it. To smell it. Nothing compared to the feeling she got from the scent of wet soil. She liked to walk across the fields at dawn to see how much her plants had grown during the night. Sometimes she liked to wander through the sown fields at night and listen carefully for the sound of the plants as they grew. Lupita could even hear the cracking of a seed in the ground as it gave way to a new sprout.

No one believed it, and she hadn't spoken of it for years. Her mother's family had migrated from the country, and during childhood summers she visited the relatives that had stayed behind at their farm, where she contributed to the daily labor. Forces outside of her control had made her a city mouse, but if she could have chosen she definitely would have lived in the country.

Because of her family history she had no trouble adapting to life in an indigenous community nestled within the mountainous state of Guerrero. Or at least that's where she had been told she was. Her exact location was a mystery, but it didn't concern her in the slightest. She remembered spending hours in the back of a vehicle driven by her silent savior, the man who'd rescued her off the street but hadn't uttered a word during their entire journey. She only knew his name: Tenoch. Lupita had stared at his unusual piercings, which matched the description she had given her superiors for the suspect's sketch. Was it a coincidence? Or had Lupita become a magnet for these kinds of people? Her discomfort was greater than her curiosity, so she decided to keep quiet and lie down in the backseat with her eyes closed. The vibration of the car indicated that they had been on a highway for a long time before driving along a dirt road. She wouldn't have wished that on her worst enemy. The pain in her leg and ribs got worse with every bump. Finally, at dawn, they reached their destination. Tenoch killed the engine, got out of the car, opened the back door, and offered Lupita his hand.

"Where are we?" asked Lupita.

"In a safe place."

Lupita tried to observe her surroundings, but thick fog didn't let her see more than two feet. A pack of dogs barked. An indigenous woman came out of a hut and walked toward them with a sarape in her hand. She wrapped Lupita in it and gently led her to another cabin, where a cot was waiting for her. A few moments later another woman came in and offered Lupita a cup of tea. Lupita drank it, lay back, and immediately fell asleep. Later on, the cold woke her. She tried to search for covers and the cot creaked.

"Are you cold?" asked a woman's voice.

"Yes."

"We'll get you a cup of coffee."

Lupita could see nothing in the darkness. When the light of day finally came through the cracks of the wooden hut's walls Lupita learned that she had shared the space with three other women who had already begun to get ready. One ground corn for the tortillas. Another lit a fire and made coffee for everyone. The third left to get eggs for breakfast.

From the day she arrived these women showered Lupita with attention and care. They offered her everything they had without hesitation. She never felt like an outsider. The smell of the fresh handmade tortillas sparked her appetite. Lupita happily ate a scrambled egg and a couple of tortillas, and drank a cup of coffee. Later on she would learn that she had been fed an egg because of her delicate health, but the community could not always afford the luxury of eating eggs for breakfast.

Women and children composed the community. Tenoch—the man who had brought her there—had disappeared the day after their arrival and had not been seen again. The women of the community were perfectly organized and were very hard workers. Lupita once asked about the men and was told they either had migrated or were employed by drug cartels. Because of this, the majority of the population were women, children, and elders.

"And where are the men who work for the cartels?" asked Lupita.

"Who cares? We don't want them here; they endanger us."

The women told Lupita that one day, tired of living in anxiety, they spoke to the Council of Elders and they all decided they would no longer tolerate hit men, drug traffickers, and addicts. It was decided that anyone who violated these terms and affected the community would be banned forever.

"They just up and left?"

"No, of course not. We had to put up a fight, and the community police from Paraíso helped us out."

"What do you mean community police? How does that work?"

"They're all indigenous like us and they want the same things we do. They receive no salary for their work, and they risk their lives defending us from abuse, from the government, the federal police, the army, and the cartels. They have taught us to organize with our own resources and to protect our own, as they have done for over eighteen years. They were also sick of so much death in their town and the cartels' way of ruling, so they gathered their grandparents' rifles from the Revolution and they killed the narcos."

"Just like that?"

"What other way is there? Dead dogs don't bite."

"But there's a lot of rabid dogs out there, and they're well organized," Lupita said.

"You're right, and it's not easy. Hit men come every once in a while to scare us into planting their drugs, but when we see them approaching we ask for help and the community police always come."

"To kill them all, I assume."

"Correct."

"That's kind of rough, don't you think?"

"What they do is worse. Look ma'am, those narcos that mutilate, torture, and kill others are no longer a part of us. They're no longer part of any family or community; they act against everyone. They are worth nothing. But when you bury a narco, you allow him to be a part of you again. He becomes dust, food, our brother once more. His body—dissolved in the earth—now sustains life again, instead of destroying it."

ALCOHOLISM IN ANCIENT MEXICO

Before the arrival of the Spaniards to what is now considered Mexico, alcoholism was not a health issue among the indigenous population. Its consumption was heavily regulated. The ingestion of pulque, the fermented drink distilled from the maguey cactus, was only allowed for people older than fifty-two and elite priests during special ceremonies. Regular citizens could only drink it during the holidays. Public inebriation was severely punished. If someone acted drunk in public they risked being beaten to death. In the pre-Hispanic peoples' cosmogony—

in which every life has a purpose—
alcoholics deserved death because they
had surrendered their will to the wrong
deity, which became an impediment for
the fulfillment of their plan. The only
ones allowed to drink without restriction
were those whose active lives were over
and thus would not become a burden on
society or a hindrance to the cosmic order.

In the first recorded governmental
speech to the people, alcoholic beverages
were referred to as "the beginning of all
evil and perdition, because *octli* [pulque
in the Náhuatl tongue] is like an infernal
tempest that unites all evil. From drunken-
ness come robbery, theft, and violence . . .
the drunkard finds no rest in peace and
quiet. Their mouths do not speak peaceful
or temperate words. The drunkard is the
destruction of public peace."

Lupita remained in silence after what she had heard. Nobody had ever said anything similar to her before. This concept of life and death called for reflection. She wondered what Carmela—the woman who had been explaining everything—would think of her if she found out Lupita was an alcoholic who cared for no one else when she was inebriated.

"The man who brought me here, is he part of the community police?" Lupita asked.

"Tenoch? No way! He's our shaman; he heals and protects our souls," said Carmela.

"So where is he?"

"In the capital. He has great work to do there, and we have a lot of work to do here, so excuse me, I need to leave for the field."

"Yes, please, go. Wait, how do you communicate when you need to call for help? My phone is dead and I need to make a call."

"You'll have to wait for the shaman or his mother, who is also a shaman. They will come back for a baptism in a couple of weeks and they have a cell phone."

Lupita pondered the conversation. She knew about the good work that the community police in Guerrero had been doing. She also knew that they had tried to be recognized by the authorities for years so that they could guard their communities and uphold justice according to their own traditions. But she had never heard of it first-hand. The police she knew of mostly protected criminals and dishonest politicians. Very rarely did they care about normal citizens. Lupita wished she were part of the community police, to serve others and risk her life for a greater cause. She felt that by leaving her police uniform behind at home she had left behind the negative aspect of her job and was remembering the true purpose that had driven her to become a policewoman.

Lupita wanted to tell these women that she was a police officer and could help protect the community. She wanted to show gratitude for their kindness and generosity, but now wasn't the right time. In her present state she couldn't even defend an ant. First she had to mend her physical condition and heal the most sensitive—and damaged—part of her being. Also, she liked the idea of living in anonymity. These women knew nothing about her; they didn't judge or reject her. They knew nothing of her past so they could not reproach her. For them she was an ordinary woman who needed help, and they obliged generously. What was surprising was that they cared for her without neglecting their duties. Their community was organized under the structure of *tequio*, in which every inhabitant of the community contributes to the well-being of the group through work. It was a genuinely positive form of collaboration. No one expected compensation other than the satisfaction of elevating the quality of life for every single member of the community.

That same structure guaranteed the efficiency of the community police. It was the exact opposite of the political and work environments Lupita had known her whole life, where nobody ever volunteered for anything or shared without expecting something in return. It was obvious that a tremendous social decay had permeated political parties and government offices in Mexico's capital. But in this place—away from "civilization"—all she witnessed from the moment she opened her eyes until she closed them at night was the overwhelming beauty of a mountain range that was blanketed by fog at night and completely uncovered in the morning. It was a spectacle of such beauty that it moved Lupita to tears. She considered it a privilege to watch from her cot the magic moment in which the mist dispersed and the mountains appeared.

Nature, along with the generous gestures of the indigenous women, finally allowed Lupita to comprehend the idea of a superior power, a supreme energy that organized the movement of the stars, that regulated ecosystems and that—among many other things—synchronized the cycles of women with the cycles of the moon.

Lupita's soul healed day by day, as did her broken bones. When her leg was strong enough to support her she liked to take night strolls through the moonlit fields. Even though it was night she wore a broad hat because she had heard from her grandmother that moonlight is just as powerful as sunlight, and one should take precautions before being exposed to it. She liked knowing that from the darkness of the soil, life could erupt. That even though she couldn't see them in plain sight, there were seeds that germinated, opened, grew, and would become a part of us. There are things that can't be seen but exist nonetheless.

Just as congressmen and senators had taken advantage of the darkness of dawn to hastily approve reforms and come to infamous, cowardly, and ignominious agreements that would hand over her country's natural resources to foreign entities, Lupita learned that there was another Mexico where new seeds were being sown, seeds that were still invisible but would soon bear fruit to new ideas, new organizations, a new sense of community.

As the days passed Lupita felt less need to speak to Celia or Captain Martinez. Insisting was of no use. Her phone's battery was long dead, and there was no way to charge it. That was that. So she fully immersed herself in the lessons that isolation was giving her. One of the greatest benefits of this isolation was that it calmed her consumerist anxiety. People in big cities enter a vortex of consumption even without wanting to: the newest smartphone, the newest iPad, the newest sound system, the newest way to stream movies, the newest microwave oven. It took longer to acquire these products than for them to be replaced by a new model. In the face of the inability to acquire new devices, people lived in a constant state of dissatisfaction. Now she realized that she really didn't give a rat's ass if she owned the smartest phone.

Lupita also learned to enjoy the new things that nature offered, things that required no purchase. The newest sunset, the newest shoots of a tree, the first drop of dew. Everything was novel. Everything changed day to day. Everything transformed, free of charge.

After twenty-one days of this emotional cleansing—of not reading newspapers, of not being aware of the government's treacheries, of not bearing witness to death—Lupita felt part of a spirit that envelops everything, that renews everything. And just as the mist disappeared in the mornings among the tall mountains, so did the dense shroud of sadness disperse from Lupita's heart.

LUPITA LIKED TO PROTECT

Maybe that was why she became a policewoman. It gave her great satisfaction to help out in an emergency, to provide support, to care for and comfort others.

In the building where she grew up her friends always had asked her to defend them. Celia was the one who most often had come to her for help. Celia was three years younger than Lupita and had been a small and skittish girl. She was terrified of Doña Toña's turkeys, which were often loose and unattended in the building's courtyard, and would peck the girls when they were playing. As soon as Lupita saw the turkeys get agitated she used her body as a shield to protect Celia.

A smile formed on Lupita's lips. It had been so long since she'd reminisced about her childhood games! Sometimes it was even hard for her to remember that she had once been a happy girl. Lupita had laughed contagiously, and when they were girls, Celia and she often fell into fits of laughter. If Doña Trini was around, she would say, "Stop laughing so much, you look stupid." That would only make them laugh harder. They laughed so much together! As Lupita grew she lost that childish joy, but she kept her vigorous laughter. No one could hear her laugh without joining in. Of course, her best echo always came from Celia. So they faced the turkeys many times, just for laughs. These acts of courage had resulted in innumerable pecks, but she never wavered. The satisfaction Lupita had gotten from providing protection to friends and neighbors was greater than the pain in her legs from the pecking.

Life in the community had been calm even though the rest of the state of Guerrero was in turmoil. Lupita was now completely assimilated to her new life. She loved to be awakened by the roosters and to hear the birds sing and chirp during her morning activities, especially a flock that flew out of a cave when the first rays of sunlight hit the sky. To rise with the sun and to go to bed early after a long day of hard work was a blessing. Her broken leg was healing quite well. Her rib did not hurt anymore, and it had only been twenty-one days since her arrival. She was completely adapted. An outside observer would not have detected a difference between her and the rest of the women in the community. Lupita braided her hair like them and shared their features and skin color, although she was not as tan from the sun.

On this particular morning, Lupita could say she felt happy. She was using a *jícara* to take a bath next to Carmela in a small shack that served as an outdoor shower. Carmela was helping Lupita cover the cast on her leg so it wouldn't get wet. From outside of the shack they could hear the everyday sounds: children playing, chickens clucking, dogs barking.

But Lupita became alert because the dogs were barking louder than usual. She remembered the day she had arrived.

"Hey Carmela, do you think Tenoch is back?"

"Maybe. We were expecting him yesterday."

Lupita remained vigilant. She was half-dressed when she heard the dogs bark again and the sounds of people running and yelling. The two women held their breath as Lupita peeked through the shack's wooden planks. She saw several men indiscriminately hitting the women and children that were blocking the entrance to the community. Lupita felt her blood boil. She couldn't stand to watch anyone use violence against civilians. She got dressed in a hurry and silently exited the shack without being seen by the attackers.

This group of five armed men had fled from a town in the state of Michoacán, where they had been involved in a shoot-out against an *Autodefensa* group. Autodefensa groups were different from the community police, but they also emerged from the people's need to defend themselves against organized crime's constant bullying and demands for payoffs—and the constant kidnappings, rapes, and homicides—since the official police were never of any help and often colluded with the narcos. Several Autodefensa groups had been expanding and taking over towns in Michoacán, recovering control of their lands and participating in the election of their authorities. Many of these groups were inspired by the Zapatista movement, which had achieved a great deal in its twenty years of existence. To begin with, Autodefensa groups worked their own lands and were self-sufficient. They now controlled twenty-seven autonomous municipalities in which alcohol and other drugs were banned. Justice was carried out in their territories without government interference. Women were respected, occupied important positions, and took on hard-earned responsibilities. Within the territories they occupied, Autodefensa groups were the law and decided their own destiny.

Now, gunshots rang out from afar. Despite her limp, Lupita immediately found herself in the epicenter of the action. One of the hit men was pointing his weapon at an old man, who cursed at him in his indigenous tongue. Lupita snuck up behind the criminal and struck him in the back of the neck with her cane. The man keeled over.

Lupita grabbed his gun and shot at the rest of the hit men, wounding two and scattering the rest, all of this while hopping on her one good leg. As soon as the attackers left, Lupita collapsed on the dirt, totally drained. She realized that the members of the community were looking at her with gratitude in their eyes. One of Carmela's daughters approached her and hugged her fondly. Lupita felt very satisfied.

Just as everyone was surprised at her courage and the speed with which she responded to the aggression, she was surprised to observe that the weapon she had taken from the man whose neck she had broken was a Xiuhcóatl rifle. She couldn't make sense of how these criminals were in possession of weaponry exclusive to the Special Forces of the Mexican Army. The Xiuhcóatl ("fire serpent" in the Náhuatl tongue) was an assault rifle designed by the General Directorate of Military Industry of the Army.

XIUHCÓATL: FIRE SERPENT, SOLAR SERPENT

Xiuhcóatl was the most powerful weapon of the Aztec gods. It was an atlatl—or spear thrower—that belonged to Huitzilopochtli (the sun), who was born to Coatlicue (the earth goddess). According to myth, a ball of feathers impregnated Coatlicue when it fell on her breast while she was sweeping. When she finished sweeping she tried to remove the feathers, but they were gone. She then learned of her pregnancy. Her previous four hundred sons and her daughter, Coyolxauhqui, felt shamed. They did not approve of their mother's pregnancy and decided to murder her. They set forth under Coyolxauhqui's orders and as they were about to reach their mother, Huitzilopochtli was born. He dressed himself in fine feathers, took Xiuhcóatl in his hands, and used it to decapitate his sister. Coyolxauhqui rolled down a mountain and was dismembered. Then Huitzilopochtli annihilated his four hundred brothers. When he was done he took his sister's head and flung it into the sky, and it became the moon, thus symbolizing the eternal struggle between the sun and the moon. Human sacrifices in honor of Huitzilopochtli were carried out in Tenochtitlán with the purpose of giving him vigor so that he could continue his battle against darkness, and thus assuring the sun would again rise every fifty-two years.

Lupita was sure that the man she had killed was not part of the military. His movements did not match those of a man trained in the armed forces. Where could he and his comrades have obtained the rifle? Did they have dealings with nearby military groups? There was no way to know. What she did know was that she urgently needed to call Celia to tell her she was alive, that she had survived once more. Poor Celia. She probably thought Lupita was dead!

On Holy Friday, a day after Celia had checked her friend into rehab and the day of the attack on the rehab facility, Lupita's apartment had been broken into. The apartment building had been desolate, as everyone was outside watching the Passion procession. There were no witnesses. When Celia returned home she noticed that Lupita's door was open. At first she assumed Lupita had escaped from rehab and had come back home. But when she entered the apartment and found it trashed, she realized someone had broken in. No electronics had been stolen. It seemed like whoever broke in had been looking for something in particular. Celia immediately headed to the police station to report the break-in, but the officer on duty was so sleep deprived that he gave every sort of excuse to avoid opening a case. First he told her that since she wasn't the owner of the apartment they couldn't begin an investigation or even take her statement unless she brought a signed power of attorney, proof of residence, a copy of her official ID, and the most recent energy bill. Fortunately Captain Martinez appeared and took Celia by the arm, gently leading her to his office, where Celia learned about the attack on the rehab facility. The captain gave her a preliminary report regarding fatalities and casualties. Before Celia passed out, he assured her that Lupita wasn't on either list. She was missing. He asked Celia if she knew where Lupita could be.

"That's what I want to know!" Celia shouted. "I checked her into that place, and you are the only one who knew she was there. And, and then gunmen immediately shot it up?"

"Are you trying to pin this on me?"

Celia shrugged, dazed and upset.

"Look Celia, I did go try to find Lupita, but I arrived just after the shooting," Martinez said, staring off into space before returning his gaze to Celia. "I don't owe you any explanations! I'm the detective, and I ask the questions. Do you or don't you know where your friend is?"

"I don't."

"Thank you. You can leave."

Celia got up and headed for the door, but before she left, Martinez added, thinking of the relationship that had been sparked at the dance hall, "For your information, I am very invested in finding Lupita."

The captain and Celia weren't the only ones looking for Lupita. Apparently a group tied to Mami's illicit activities was actively searching for her as well. Martinez hoped to find Lupita alive before the people who attacked the rehab facility got to her. He didn't buy the official version: that the attackers were taking revenge on former addicts who no longer consumed drugs sold by Mami. He was sure that there was something else going on, and Lupita could lead them to capture the perpetrators. There was no doubt that Mami was somehow behind it all, but he needed proof to build a case. Mami, on the other hand, was recovering beautifully.

The Passion procession was over and everything was back to normal, but it had left a bitter aftertaste in the delegación. This festivity had been carried out for over one hundred years with the full cooperation of all eight neighborhoods of Iztapalapa. It was a prime example of true civilian efforts. The authorities only provided protection and support; everything else was handled by the inhabitants of the delegación, and this was the first year that the event had been stained by violence.

LUPITA LIKED TO DEDUCE

To analyze, review, and read reality through her particular method of observation. The conclusions she arrived at were surprising. With very little information—hints that would go by unnoticed by most people—Lupita could solve any kind of mystery. Nothing brought her more joy than tying up loose ends. Putting together a puzzle, placing the last piece, was something she greatly enjoyed. Her favorite puzzles were the ones that had thousands of pieces. She would assemble them on her dining table and her obsessive personality glued her to the chair until she was either finished or had to go to work. She could stay up for several nights if necessary, and if she slept at all, her dreams were about where a particular piece might fit. The delegado's death had affected her in the same manner. Her mind kept analyzing the event from different vantage points. In her mind, Lupita had seen the delegado die hundreds of times, in slow motion, in fast motion, forward and backward. She could account for everything that had happened, or at least what she thought had happened, second by second. But in the end she really knew nothing.

The arrival of Tenoch to the community gave her an opportunity to communicate with the outside world and to collect the data she lacked to clear her thoughts and get rid of the mental torment she had endured the past weeks. It was a bright day. Lupita felt calm in spite of the previous day's turmoil that had left one man dead. A car arrived, welcomed by the dogs' joyous barking. Tenoch was driving. Conchita Ugalde, his mother, rode in the front passenger seat. In the backseat was a man Lupita didn't know.

Lupita was surprised by the affection and respect that the women of the community showed Conchita. To her Conchita was only the bathroom attendant at the dance hall, and nothing else. She never knew that Conchita was a revered shaman and that Tenoch was her son.

The perception she'd had of Conchita was so far from reality that Lupita took it as further proof that she couldn't trust what her eyes saw. Conchita greeted her warmly, with her usual deference, as always. Carmela looked at Lupita with admiration upon learning she was a friend of Conchita's. Tables were set up outside the huts and a breakfast of tamales and coffee was organized for the recently arrived guests. Tenoch spoke words of gratitude for the food and then introduced Salvador Camarena, his friend and collaborator. During breakfast Tenoch and Conchita learned of the previous day's events. A grave had been dug for the dead hit man, but the community was awaiting instructions before proceeding. Tenoch checked with Conchita and immediately told the community members that the first step was to have a purification ceremony, then a healing session for anyone whose emotions were altered from the recent events.

After breakfast was over and everyone had expressed their gratitude, they all rose from the table and began to prepare for the ceremonies. Lupita asked Carmela how she could be of help. Carmela told her that in her condition the most she could do was help iron the clothing that would be worn during the ritual. Lupita could not think of a more fitting duty.

She set up in the center of the hut to iron the clothing she was given. It was quite complicated because in this community they used a coal iron. Fortunately Lupita knew how to work it. As she lit the fire to heat up the coal she thought that if she had a steam iron she could finish a lot faster, but it was a pointless thought since the community had no electricity. The women here preferred tools that could be used anywhere and under any circumstance. These communities often had to mobilize to avoid attacks from the drug cartels and when they fled they took only the most essential possessions. They had to remain unseen, hidden. That was why they didn't use cell phones either, to avoid being tracked by satellites. They lived a simple life, very close to nature. Lupita had truly rediscovered the pleasures of sowing, reaping, capturing rainwater, and of recovering her health by using medicinal plants. Herbal medicine was an important tradition filled with ancestral knowledge passed down orally, and it was vital in locations that had no doctors. The women here had shown her how they healed each other using the curative powers of plants, and they had shared the knowledge inherited from generations of wise men and women who heard and saw much more than the senses allow.

Lupita had already seen for herself the importance of such knowledge. She'd assisted a traditional midwife during a birth, and it was an experience she would never forget. Two women from a nearby community had arrived seeking help; a woman in their village was about to give birth. The child was breech, and no one in the village knew about that type of delivery. That morning most women were out tending the fields, so Lupita offered to help the midwife. They immediately left for the neighboring community, traveling by donkey. When Lupita learned that the young woman in labor had blood pressure issues, she thought the worst, but it didn't even faze the midwife. She took a piece of cloth, tore it, and gave it to Lupita to tie around the woman's thigh, to be tightened or loosened when she gave the order. That was how they controlled the pregnant woman's blood pressure. The midwife very skillfully turned the child around so it could be born, and asked if there were any scissors to cut the umbilical cord. She was told there was nothing there but an old beer bottle. The midwife smashed the bottle against the wall, picked up a piece of glass, and ran it over a lit candle, the only means of sterilization at hand. Then she used it to cut the cord. There on that dirt floor, Lupita had witnessed the miracle of life. The great mystery. The approximation to light. The birth of light.

That day a memory crept around the corners of Lupita's mind, a memory she couldn't quite place. The sound of the bottle breaking tried to establish a connection in her head but didn't quite accomplish it. Lupita had to concentrate the totality of her five senses on the task at hand, so she couldn't dwell on the memory. She didn't realize it at the time, but that sound was a piece in the puzzle she had to put together to solve the delegado's death.

It was a sound, a simple sound that would make sense when the time came. Every sound announces movement. A dog barking announces someone's arrival. The crackle of fire on a stove is the sign of energy in motion. The ringing of a phone is the resonance of a person's thoughts trying to reach another, to listen to them, to know of them, to do away with distance.

Lupita asked Tenoch to let her charge her phone. He started his car and plugged in the charger. When Lupita's phone turned back on she saw on the screen several lost calls and messages from Celia and Captain Martinez. Her eyes filled with tears. She called her friend first.

"Celia?"

"Lupita?"

"Yes."

The moment she heard her friend's voice, Celia couldn't hold back the tears. "Oh, mana! I thought you were dead!"

"I know. That's why I'm calling . . . Don't cry, Celia, I'm okay. How are you? I'm also worried about you."

"You had me worried sick! Where are you?"

"In a safe place."

Lupita was surprised to hear herself use the same phrase that Tenoch had said to her the day he'd delivered her to the community. Now she understood the importance of no one knowing the community's exact location. Lupita and Celia spoke for quite a while. Celia broke her own record for number of words spoken without stopping to catch her breath. Lupita heard all about how the Passion procession went well in spite of everything, and that Don Neto—the Judas understudy—had handled the insults from the crowd and only lost his temper toward the end, almost coming to blows with some guy. The car washer's wig stayed on the whole time. The main actors' makeup withstood the heat, and so on and so forth. Finally Celia told Lupita that her apartment had been broken into and that Mami's henchmen were staking out her house. Celia also told Lupita that Captain Martinez was looking for her, but she expressed her doubts about the captain's innocence in the attack on the rehab facility. Lupita immediately defended him. Her desire to be right pushed her to vouch for the man she was so attracted to. As soon as she got off the phone with Celia she called Martinez, and when she heard his voice, her heart skipped a beat. His voice reflected sincerity, and it was plainly evident that the captain was very glad to hear from her.

"Señorita Lupita, I'm so glad to hear from you."

"Thanks. But are we still on formal terms after the other night?"

"Ha ha, sorry but I'm from the north, and you know that's how we address each other. How are you?"

"Very well, recovering."

"I'm happy to hear that. I've been thinking of you. You had me worried."

"Well, thank God I'm all right and getting better."

"Where are you, if I may ask?"

Lupita thought for a second before she answered. Celia's doubts about the captain had gotten to her.

"You don't have to tell me if you don't want to," Martinez said, sensing her hesitation. "It's better that you don't mention it over the phone, just to be safe. What's important is that you're okay and getting better. I just wanted to know how you were doing because I was starting to fear the worst. Your call has made my day. You know I'm at your command and ready to help you any way I can."

"Thank you."

"You're welcome. Call me when you get the chance; we have to go dancing again."

"Thank you, thank you. I'll call when I can."

After ending the call with Martinez, Lupita's brain kicked into high gear. On one hand it was now clear to her that Martinez hadn't sold her out to whoever had attacked the rehab facility. If he were an informant, he would have insisted on knowing her location. On the contrary, he wanted to protect her. Her heart was happily pumping blood, and that allowed her to make the right connections and deduce at an incredible speed. If Mami had given the order to break into her apartment, it was because she was after something important, something Lupita had. Something that Mami didn't want out in the open. Lupita didn't remember telling Mami that she was in possession of incriminating evidence against her. She had been completely drunk when she'd said that. What could hurt Mami? She was a powerful person who enjoyed absolute impunity. Every public servant who had occupied an elected position in the delegación government in recent years had gotten most of their votes thanks to her, and they protected her even though they were well aware of her illegal activities. And no matter how much it pained her, Lupita included Larreaga on that list. All evidence indicated that he had made a pact with Mami. But what did Lupita have to do with any of it? What could she know? What could she say that would hurt Mami?

Even Lupita often overlooked when street vendors pretended to sell fake artisan pieces but actually sold drugs. It was pointless to try to arrest them when the highest authorities protected them. She mostly tried to avoid them and barely acknowledged their presence. Though she had to admit that in the past weeks she not only had come in contact with them but she also had bought drugs from them. Of course! If a series of events transpire around a specific person, it means that person is the guiding force behind those events. That meant Lupita was that loose thread in this fabric of corruption that encompassed the public service and the street vendors. If Mami was still looking for her, it meant she hadn't found what she was looking for. Whatever it was, it was still in Lupita's possession. What did she have with her? She had escaped the attack on the rehab facility in nothing but a hospital gown. Wait! She had her phone! Lupita had surrendered all her possessions when she checked in to rehab. But once she was in her own room, she'd asked for her phone back. Celia refused, because part of the program required patients to go through a period of isolation. Lupita had begged Celia, saying she would hide it inside her cast and no one would know. Celia agreed and Lupita kept her word. She carefully hid it in her cast and only used it at night. She didn't really need to talk to anyone, but she was addicted to a farming video game. Thanks to her video-game addiction, Lupita had kept her phone with her. There had to be vital information on it.

Lupita felt proud of herself for escaping the shoot-out with the device, but she regretted not bringing the charger. She could have come to a quicker conclusion. Funny enough, since Lupita had come to the community she hadn't felt the need to play her farm game. Her poor animals must've been starving. She turned the phone back on and began to look for any useful information. Other than missed calls and text messages from Celia, Martinez, and some other acquaintances, there were some voice mails from her superiors on the police force, asking her to show up for duty immediately. The last one was Chief Arévalo angrily informing her that she was fired.

She was surprised to hear a voice mail from Conchita Ugalde. Lupita had never received a call from her before. She remembered that the last time they had seen each other was when Lupita threw up in the dance hall bathroom. Conchita had helped her and then asked for her number, to stay in touch.

Lupita moved on to the photos but didn't find anything relevant until she went through the videos. First she played one where she recorded herself, completely drunk, about to enter a *pulquería*. She was trying to record and speak at the same time, so the image was very unsteady.

"Lupita the alkie here," she said between bouts of laughter, "reporting live from pulquería El Gatito."

"That's cute, I'm about to enter the puss . . ." Her laughter didn't let her finish the phrase.

The phone fell, and as she tried to pick it up she lost her balance and fell to the floor. She couldn't get up.

"Fuuuuuck, that hurt!"

That was the end of that video. The following videos were just as pathetic. Lupita had recorded them during her "seven cantinas tour" prior to the Passion procession. Finally, Lupita clicked on a video she had recorded at the seventh and final cantina. In the video she saw herself drink a shot of tequila, then a waiter approached and told her to stop recording. Lupita became aggressive, and she was escorted from the premises through the back door. The phone was still recording while the cantina employees tried to take it from her hands, but she held them back with what seemed like flying kicks. She was finally thrown to the curb and as Lupita fell the images on the video became a flurry of confusion: lights, hands, feet, cement, shoes. "Come on you motherfuckers!" she screamed. "You don't want me to record? I'm Lupita the alkie! Queen of undercover reporting! I'll record the fuck out of you *putitos*."

The next video showed Lupita crawling, her drunk face in the foreground as she slowly said, "What is this?" She had turned her phone around so the camera focused on the inside of a basement—shot through a small ground-level window. A group of men were counting cash and stuffing it in empty shoe boxes. From the video Lupita could tell she had adjusted her position and zoomed in. She must have rested the phone against something because the image became stabilized and fixed. Just then Mami entered the basement. Gonzalo Lugo walked toward her and offered his arm. They walked close to the window to have a conversation away from the rest of the people and, unknowingly, closer to Lupita's camera.

"So, Lugo, how much did you come up with?"

"Only fifty million pesos."

"That's not nearly enough. For a political campaign like the one Gomez is planning we will spend that much every day! Let me remind you we're not just talking about a fucking delegación, he plans to run for mayor of Mexico City after that."

"I know boss, but drug sales have been slipping."

"What do you mean slipping? Drugs don't sell themselves! We sell them, and your people aren't doing it fast enough."

"Well, two of our dealers left us to join Salvador."

"Have you talked to this Salvador? What does he want? What's his price?"

"I talked to him, but he's dead set on his warriors of light bullshit and isn't cooperating."

"Then send him a message, *cabrón*. It's not like you're new to this. We can't let this opportunity pass us by. Did you give Gomez the money personally?"

"Yes, along with your message."

The last phrase was muted by the sound of Lupita throwing up. Mami, alarmed, said, "Who's out there? Go check it out, *pendejos*! Hurry!"

The video ended. That's what Mami was after! Everything was starting to make sense. This video was very important. Lupita had to guard it carefully. Her analytic mind was spinning like crazy. In his conversation with Mami, Gonzalo Lugo had mentioned some guy named Salvador. A few minutes earlier, when Lupita walked to get her phone from her hut so she could charge it with Tenoch, she had crossed paths with Salvador, the shaman's friend and guest. Salvador had been sitting on the ground surrounded by a group of children. He was teaching them how to carve obsidian. Next to him was a sack with obsidian pieces of all sizes, and he was handing them out along with gloves to protect their hands. Lupita had thought, *Good, glass shards can really hurt.* Lupita had seen the children making arrows before. They all practiced shooting them with a bow, not so much as a war strategy but as a sport. Cartel hit men attacked their communities with powerful weaponry, but they fought back with weapons of a different sort. Salvador had waved at her and Lupita waved back. Salvador asked how her rib was doing and Lupita said it was much better, but then she asked, "How do you know my rib was broken?"

"I work at the rehab facility where you were admitted. I signed your admission form."

They talked briefly about the attack and about the police investigation it caused, but Lupita was in a hurry to charge her phone so she politely excused herself and went on her way. Was this the same Salvador who was stealing Mami's men and recruiting them to his ranks?

Carmela, who asked if she was done ironing the clothes, interrupted Lupita's deep thoughts. Lupita apologized. The clothes would be ready soon since the coals were now hot enough for the iron.

The first thing that caught Lupita's attention was the smell of Conchita's white huipil. It smelled like powdered soap. It was freshly washed but hadn't been dried out in the sun correctly. Lupita was now used to the pleasant smell of the indigenous women's clothes. They smelled of burnt firewood, of sun and mountain breeze. Tenoch's and Conchita's clothing smelled of city. She was done with the huipil in just five minutes and continued with Tenoch's shirt. When she smoothed it out on the table she realized she had found the delegado's shirt! The same shirt she mentioned during her official statement at the police station, with the wrinkled collar. What was that shirt doing among Tenoch's clothes? She was sure it was the same shirt. The wrinkle on the collar was unmistakable. Lupita remembered the moment she noticed it for the first time.

She had been directing traffic outside the adult education center that the delegado was going to inaugurate. As soon as the delegado's car had arrived, Lupita showed off her skills with a whistle, trying to make an impression. The delegado was helped out of the backseat of the car by Inocencio. When Larreaga walked beside her, Lupita had noticed the deep wrinkle in his shirt collar. She harshly judged and condemned whoever had ironed the shirt. Did the delegado's wife not know how to iron? Or didn't she have someone to do it for her? It was terribly unfortunate that a politician of his stature would be photographed in a shirt in such poor condition.

Lupita ran her fingers over the shirt. The wrinkle was still there, and it wasn't necessary to wonder why it had remained for so long, especially after being washed. It was like the old saying "The more things change, the more they stay the same." Boy, did Lupita know about that!

The shirt had come into her life too late yet just in time. How could this be? She couldn't travel back in time to shove it down her superiors' throats and prove that she wasn't wrong about thinking that the missing wrinkle could be a lead. But there was still time to solve Larreaga's mysterious death. For starters, she could prove the shirt was his because his initials were embroidered on the breast pocket and that was irrefutable evidence. Lupita had to put her thoughts on hold because Carmela returned to fetch the clothes and to ask Lupita to join the purification ceremony prior to the hit man's burial. It was imperative that she attended, as she had been the one to take his life. Lupita didn't object, even though her head was filled with questions. She changed into a white huipil and braided her hair.

The ceremony proved to be very interesting. Conchita used incense to cleanse all the attendants, while a group of women sang and beat on drums. Then she passed a flower bouquet from their heads to their feet in order to free them from evil energies. Next, they wrapped the deceased's body in a shawl that served as a shroud. Finally Conchita began the ceremony with a prayer:

Sacred Mother Earth, receive this shawled
    man.
Cleanse his heart.
Open his heart.
Unclog his heart.
Let the divine nourishment you fed him
become food once again.
Let his blood and flesh become
good food.
Cut his ties to darkness with
thirteen obsidian blades.
Let this obsidian tear the black cloak
that covers his soul and let him return to
    the light

and recognize his true face.
Virgin of Guadalupe, cover him with your
  mantle
of stars and transform him into
a warrior of the light.

Conchita took an obsidian disc from her clothes and put it on the shawl that covered the corpse, over the man's heart. Then Tenoch and Salvador used ropes to lower the body into a grave while four women beat on drums. Lupita listened to the chanting, delighted. She felt like an integral part of the ceremony. Both Conchita's huipil and Tenoch's shirt looked impeccable thanks to her ironing. There was no doubt that Lupita was a true artist with an iron. As the body was being carefully lowered into the grave, the obsidian disc on the man's chest slipped and smashed into a thousand pieces against a rock. The sound the obsidian made when it broke was stowed away in Lupita's mind, and this time it was clear to her. That was one of the first puzzle pieces that found its place, triggering a series of memories of isolated events that began to fit together in her head.

LUPITA LIKED TO ASK QUESTIONS

To know the purpose behind things. To know the hidden causes that pushed people to act a certain way. What intrigued her the most was how some people were silent in the face of injustice, abuse, and illegal activities. She didn't mean how people remained passive about acts of corruption but how they overlooked actions carried out by people close to them, in their everyday lives, knowing said actions were affecting the lives of many others. For example, she didn't understand how a woman could ever live with a rapist husband, covering up his crime and never turning him in. Or how people knew that there was a kidnapped person in their neighbor's house but said nothing out of fear. She didn't understand why no one tried to get to the bottom of why people consume drugs. Jailing addicts or using police repression would never mitigate illegal drug trafficking. Had nobody thought to analyze the fact that their neighbors to the north consume most of the drugs produced in the world? Why do they medicate themselves so much? She had her own answers for this. For many years, the only option she had at her disposal to prevent things from happening was to not see them, to not hear them, to not be present. That's why she took drugs. What do the millions of people who consume drugs want to avoid? What do they expect to find when they leave their bodies? What do they seek so desperately? Is it the spirit? Or maybe an essence not contained within the tons of consumer products they accumulate endlessly?

Since she had been living in the countryside her head had been filled with new questions. Why should she keep working for a police force that didn't really protect the people? Why be under the orders of corrupt elected officials? Why separate her trash and recycling if the truck that came to collect it would mix it again? Why use soaps that contaminate rivers? Why keep buying and buying and buying so much shit? Now that she only possessed the bare necessities, she was finding another meaning to her existence. But, at the same time, she had more questions than ever.

In her search for answers she approached Tenoch when he was alone. The shaman was storing the objects he had used during the ritual ceremony in a satchel. Lupita sat next to him and began her good-intentioned interrogation.

"Excuse me Tenoch, may I ask a few questions?"

"As many as you like."

Lupita didn't know how to begin her inquiries, so she shot out a couple of inconsequential questions while she got her thoughts in order.

"Who named you Tenoch?"

"My mom."

"Why?"

"I don't know. I think she dreamt it."

TENOCH

Tenoch was the name of an Aztec commander who began the Age of *Huey Tlatoanis*. He was tasked with the very first Ceremony of the New Fire in 1351. It was held at a spot close to Star Hill. In his honor, the city of Cuahumixtitlan changed its name to Tenochtitlán in 1376.

"Why was that obsidian disc put on his chest before you buried him?"

"So he would return to the light."

"Why?"

"Because if he doesn't, we won't either."

"I don't understand."

"What don't you understand?"

"What does he have to do with us?"

"We were woven together."

"By whom?"

"The Universe. Everything is linked. Everything goes together. If someone is disconnected and gets loose, they alter the order of The Whole. That man had forgotten who he was. He didn't remember. He lived in the dark."

"But he's dead. With or without a ceremony, the earth would have received and recycled him."

"He wasn't only a body, was he?"

"I don't know."

"His body carried out his orders, but he couldn't govern himself. Look, we, like our forebears, believe that the Universe has a purpose and that we are part of that purpose. Everything that we do has to be aligned with the purpose to keep the balance between light and dark, day and night, life and death. If we ignore that cosmic plan, we will cause an imbalance that will affect not only our life, but also the life of the entire Universe. You can see for yourself how in recent times we have caused ecological, economic, and social disasters because the darkness—in its attempt to defeat light and cover everything—seeks out those who live without a purpose and outside of the cosmic order. The man we buried had forgotten he was a part of us. He had a false image of himself. He was looking into a black mirror, and that is the reason for the obsidian disc."

"You gave him a black mirror so he could see his light? I don't understand."

"Darkness is not the absence of light."

"I still don't get it."

"Obsidian reflects light because it contains light. We use the sharp obsidian to cut through the darkness and liberate the light. Obsidian mirrors are used with that purpose. To see our dark side but also come in contact with our luminous side."

"Is that why you killed the delegado with an obsidian disc?"

Tenoch kept quiet for a few seconds. "Yes."

"So the Universe called for the delegado's death?"

"Although you say it with sarcasm, yes. It did. In our country there are more and more people who are disconnected from everything. The use of drugs produces disconnection. The money obtained from illegal drug sales is used to create further separation, more chaos and destruction. People—without becoming conscious of it—seek to reconnect with The Whole by using drugs to escape their bodies. But instead of returning to the universal energy they become more disconnected because they use artificial drugs instead of sacred plants. They seek dealers instead of shamans. It's time for change. We must work for the light. We must return to it and connect to it, ignite the sun in our hearts. Our ancestors handed down the knowledge to conduct the Ceremony of the New Fire, which corresponds to the movements of the stars in the sky with harmony and the equilibrium of forces. The place where it must be performed is a site close to Star Hill. It's a sacred location, and it has to be there."

"And it's no longer possible to have the ceremony there because Larreaga handed over the land to Mami so she can build a tourist trap mall where her people will also distribute drugs."

"Exactly."

"Did the delegado's betrayal make him deserve death?"

"Death doesn't exist."

"Well my son died in my arms," Lupita said sarcastically.

"That doesn't mean he's dead."

"He's not?" she continued with her sarcastic tone. "Where is he then?"

"In every particle of the Universe. In the invisible. I know the fact that you can't see him seems intolerable, but that's not what hurts you the most."

"It isn't?"

"No. What hurts you the most is that you haven't apologized to him for killing him."

Lupita's eyes peeled wide open with surprise. "Did Celia tell you this?"

"Who's Celia?"

"Never mind."

"Nobody told me. The Mayans were right when they said that the cosmos is a resonating womb and that if we connect to it through the umbilical cord of the Universe we can access all the information we want. That's what I do. I connect. Would you like to connect to your son?"

"Can you teach me to do that?"

"I can guide you. Everything else you must do on your own."

Lupita remained silent for a few minutes. Her heart was beating rapidly. It seemed incredible that there could be a way for her to talk to her son, to give him all the kisses she owed him, to show him the profound sadness she felt, her pain and regret. To do that meant she would have to trust a confessed murderer, a man who had killed another in cold blood but who was now looking into her eyes with a kindness she had never known before.

"What do I have to do?"

"Participate in a ritual."

"I'll do whatever you say, but first tell me how you shot an obsidian disc at the delegado's neck."

Tenoch smiled. He got up and beckoned Lupita to follow him. He led her to his hut, where he picked up a satchel and pulled out a wooden artifact. It was some sort of slingshot with thick rubber bands, elongated and flat, that could be hidden under a long sleeve and triggered by a simple motion of the opposite hand. Lupita and Tenoch stepped outside so he could demonstrate. He placed a watermelon on a table and walked a considerable distance away from it. He then placed the slingshot on his right forearm. Following that he took an obsidian disc and placed it between the rubber bands. Tenoch raised his right arm, pointed at the watermelon, and with his left hand pulled a small trigger that fired the disc. The obsidian piece pierced the fruit effortlessly. Lupita was very surprised by the weapon's simplicity and efficacy. That was the last piece of information she needed to connect everything she had on her mind. She remembered the video Martinez had shown her in which Tenoch seemed to raise his arm to wave at the delegado. Immediately after that gesture Larreaga began to bleed out. Now she knew how he was shot and with what, but still had one question that needed to be answered.

"When and why did the Delgado give you his shirt?"

"He gave it to me so I could perform a cleansing ritual. Someone in his inner circle had told him that his chief advisor, Licenciado Gomez, I believe, had hired a dark shaman to harm him. He trusted me to protect him. He was in a hurry for my help but had no time to participate in the ceremony, so I asked for his shirt. I could cleanse the shirt and therefore cleanse him. We met in his office after he returned from the adult education center inauguration. When he was changing his shirt in the bathroom, his secretary called his phone. She talks so loud that I could hear everything she said, even through the bathroom door. She told him that she had left the documents for the expropriation of our lands on his desk for him to sign."

"So that's how you learned that he had betrayed you, and you decided to kill him."

"That's right."

"What part do I play in all of this? Why did you look after me? Why did you bring me here?"

"Because you were chosen by an obsidian shard. When my mom called me and told me you had it stuck in your finger we knew you were destined to become a warrior of the light."

"So that's why Salvador informed you as soon as I checked in to rehab?"

"Correct. You are quite the investigator."

"Thank you. By the way, a car washer also got a shard stuck in his finger."

"We have contacted him and Salvador is training him. Anything else?"

"Not for now."

Tenoch shot back: "I have a question for you."

"Yes?"

"Are you going to turn me in?"

Lupita thought it over for a split second. "No. I have a better candidate to bring to justice."

"I hope you're referring to Mami. She works for the forces of dark and is dead set on preventing the Ceremony of the New Fire because it would put an end to her business. If people find the way to reconnect with The Whole without using drugs, Mami and every other criminal organization would be doomed to death."

"Well aren't you quite the investigator?" Lupita said, smiling. "How do you know I can make a case against Mami?"

"Because her people attacked the rehab facility. At first we thought it was vengeance against former members of her organization who had deserted her to join us. But when they realized you weren't among the dead they kept looking for you, which leads us to believe that you are in possession of very important evidence against Mami and her people."

"You're right. The good news is that I'm going to put it to use, and you will be able to perform your Ceremony of the New Fire. I guarantee it."

LUPITA LIKED TO MAKE LOVE

To caress. To kiss. To hug. To lick. To moan with pleasure. To moan, moan, moan. Lupita woke up suddenly. She had been dreaming of Martinez and had an orgasm more genuine than most she had felt in her life. It was so intense that her own panting woke her. She remained still for a moment and hoped with all her soul that her roommates were still asleep. It would be very embarrassing if they had heard her.

She left the hut before the others woke up. She didn't want anyone to look her in the eye. Her face would surely betray every detail of her orgasmic dream. Lupita could still feel Martinez's breath on her neck and the pleasant sensation in her crotch. She remembered Martinez and the night they spent together, her bed creaking, and the moistness of her bedsheets. Her bedsheets! She hadn't had time to wash them. Maybe it was for the best. When she returned she would wash them with more enthusiasm. That way she could prove her theory that the loving moistness of two lovers permeates the fibers of the bedsheets and can be used as an offering to the sun. That was one of the reasons why she didn't like clothes dryers. She believed that only the sun could properly liberate the loving energy contained in the bedsheets.

Up until that day she had always thought that making love was something exclusive to couples, to bodies, to two beings that united. She had never really experienced what it was to make Love. To be Love! To be Loving energy, that which allows one to connect with water, with plants, with animals, with stars, with planets, with clouds, with rocks, with fire, with The Whole and The Nothing.

This she learned after participating in Tenoch's ceremony. It was a milestone in Lupita's life. She had no idea what was about to happen or how she would behave. All she could do was follow directions. Several members of the community had gathered deep in the jungle. Tenoch began the ritual under a tree. He saluted the four winds and invoked the grandfathers and grandmothers. Then each of the participants stepped to the center of a circle, and Tenoch offered them a pipe that contained a substance extracted from the glands of the *Bufo alvarius* toad, affectionately known as *sapito*. Of the hundreds of toad species that exist in the world, only this one—endemic to the Sonora desert—contains in its parotid glands two neurotransmitters, bufotenin and 5-methoxytryptamine, or 5-MeO-DMT, the most powerful neurotransmitter that exists in nature and which produces a hallucinogenic effect. This amphibian not only has the capacity to store vast amounts of neurotransmitters, it also has the ability to provide the enzyme that allows us to absorb them through our respiratory system without harm.

When the smoke had entered her lungs, Lupita knew everything. She saw everything. Heard everything. Understood everything, but couldn't put it in words.

In her vertiginous journey Lupita had traveled back in time before the seas separated from the skies, before rivers and mountains were formed, before the first feather covered the chest of a quetzal. Before the first turtle crossed the oceans. Before corn became the source of sustenance. Before men stopped talking to the stars. Before women invented embroidery. Before they washed and ironed their clothing. Before she was abused for the first time, before she was struck. Before she was raped. Before her son died. Before the politicians betrayed the Mexican Revolution, before the first electoral fraud, before the country was sold to foreigners. Before lines were drawn to separate countries. Before a development plan based on the exploitation of hydrocarbons was designed. Before precious metals, mines, beaches, coral reefs, diamonds, and oil were offered up for sale. Before greed dominated rulers. Before the cartels that caused so much death were created. Before death itself, before bodies, before the idea that things come to an end, before guilt, fear, and attack.

BEFORE MEXICO

She saw her entire life, from the time she was in her mother's womb to the time of her death. She saw the entire history of the Universe, from the big bang to the end of time. She saw that everything existed before rocks, rivers, and trees came to be, yet at the same time a voice inside her whispered, "Nothing exists."

The Nothing and The Whole overlapped. Things took shape and disappeared at an unusual speed. In the matter of a second, dust became malleable mud and then transformed into a mirror made of stars that burst from the big bang. Bodies of clay emerged from nothing and were as easily torn down according to the whims of the mind, but nothing was real. It was a trick, an illusion. Beyond all sound, all shapes, and all feeling there was only light. Just light. Light that reflected from everyone and everything. Lupita knew that in every reflection, she was coming home. At a certain point she couldn't tell if she was alive or dead. She was no more, she was no longer there, but at the same time she was in everything.

Nothing was hidden. Nothing hurt. The floating heads that appeared tore off their faces in front of her eyes. Her mind lost all notion of you or I. Words were erased from her tongue, and names existed no longer. Millions of particles moved at the speed of light, changing shape and color but without losing their luminous connection. She saw thousands of cables of light weave together within and without her and become part of that intergalactic fabric. She joined the vibration of thousands of violins, of infinite drums, and she traveled to the center of waves, the center of hurricanes, the center of the cross, the place where the heart of the sky meets the heart of the earth.

Planets danced in the skies. She understood that eclipses were the convergence of cycles, of times. The time of the sun and the time of the moon together formed The Whole integrated by a night sun and a day moon.

Lupita saw that which was and that which wasn't. Like when you see stars in the night sky that long ago ceased to exist.

She understood that vision had nothing to do with eyes. It was without eyes that she could truly see.

She traveled to the end of time and saw the histories of Mexico and of the entire world change. She saw people organizing differently, with a new consciousness. She saw her life become transformed completely. Lupita saw herself, in the future, threading her time with Captain Martinez's time. She saw Tenoch lighting the New Fire in his ancestors' holy land, and infinite luminous, volatile, and loving hearts emerged from that fire. Lupita saw herself loving. Loving everything and everyone. She knew she was a part of every poem, of every kiss, of every act of love. She felt love: real Love. The kind of love that makes no distinction, that doesn't separate, that is not contained within a body. She cried from so much love.

Tenoch approached her and sang in her ear while he tapped her chest lightly:

> *You must find the way*
> *to come home*
> *to reach your animal*
> *to reach your clothes*
> *to reach your outfit.*
> *Come, come.*
> *Come, don't stay in the dream.*
> *Let the four mother-angels,*
> *and the four father-angels accompany you,*
> *may you come with a serene heart,*
> *a happy heart.*
> *Come, don't stay in the dream.*

Tenoch asked Lupita to open her eyes. It had only been five minutes, but to her it had felt like eternity. She could barely raise her eyelids. Tenoch said, "Look at me."

Lupita focused her eyes but instead of seeing Tenoch she saw her own face reflected in the shaman. She turned around and was surprised to see herself not only in Tenoch but also in everyone else participating in the ceremony. She fixed her stare in Tenoch's eyes and saw in his pupil an endless tunnel, a black hole that transported her once again through different dimensions of time and space. In Tenoch's eyes she saw her son's eyes. Lupita finally understood that before her son took shape in her womb, she and he were already one, and they would forever be one. There had never been loss or separation. There had never been two separate bodies called mother and son. Lupita felt that her heart was going to explode with joy and love. She hugged Tenoch, and in his embrace she found everyone. Her mother, her father, her son, everyone whom she had loved and those she would one day love.

Lupita understood that she had never stopped loving. She had been alive since the beginning of time, and that from that moment on she had loved every time a particle connected with another. She had loved, was loving, and would love, that was a certainty. In that instant, Lupita's soul healed. Most importantly, if Lupita—who had collected so much pain, who had experienced so much anger—could heal and connect to The Whole, so could Mexico.

ABOUT THE AUTHOR

Photo © 2009 Jerry Beretta

Laura Esquivel is the award-winning author of *Like Water for Chocolate*, which has sold over four and a half million copies around the world in thirty-five languages and was adapted into a beloved film. Her other novels include *The Law of Love*, *Swift as Desire*, and *Malinche*. She lives in Mexico City.

ABOUT THE TRANSLATOR

Photo © 2015 Kelly Strawinski

Jordi Castells is a translator, graphic designer, illustrator, and producer. He has been translating at screenwriting workshops for several years, and he has illustrated novels, including Laura Esquivel's *Malinche*, and created storyboards for feature films like *Días de Gracia*. Currently his production company, Charco Creative Industries, is working on a feature documentary about music in Mexican prisons. He also adapted and illustrated a graphic novel version of this novel. He lives in Atlanta, Georgia.